"Of what are you afraid, señorita?"

Vulcan grinned at the slim bikini-clad figure facing him as he went on, "There are no sharks lurking in the depths."

"I...I can't swim," Birdie stammered, mesmerized by the dark eyes alive with devilry. "I don't know how."

"Then I will teach you." He slipped one well-tanned arm around her waist. At his touch her body stiffened and hot color suffused her cheeks. "Relax!" he admonished. "Leave yourself entirely in my hands!"

To Birdie the next minutes felt like hours. When the time came she was glad to plunge underwater just to avoid the scrutiny of his turbulent eyes.

How she ended up clinging to his lithe muscular form, coughing and sputtering, she didn't know. She *did* know there was more than one way to drown....

Castle in Spain

by

MARGARET ROME

Harlequin Books

TORONTO • LONDON • LOS ANGELES • AMSTERDAM
SYDNEY • HAMBURG • PARIS • STOCKHOLM • ATHENS • TOKYO

Original hardcover edition published in 1981
by Mills & Boon Limited

ISBN 0-373-02464-9

Harlequin edition published March 1982

CHAPTER ONE

'MENORCA is an island of peace lost in the middle
of the sea . . .' As the yacht nosed the length of a
long deep bay, seeking a berth in the charming,
bustling port of Mahon, Birdie was reminded of
Lady Daphne's enthusing when she had urged her
to leave the depressing dampness of London and
embark with herself and a mutual friend on a
cruise of the Balearics.

'I'm certain you'll find Menorca especially
appealing, my dear,' the deeply concerned widow
had insisted. 'Everyone who knows it agrees that
it possesses a certain serenity, a sense of wellbeing—*sosophrine* is the Greek word for it—
which, combined with warm sun and sea air, will
build you up physically and restore the mental
tranquillity you have temporarily lost.'

But as Birdie leant with her elbows on the rail
studying on one shore slopes of green topped by
elegant white villas each with steps descending to a
private stretch of beach; the outline of a ruined
fortress; a fishing village festooned with nets
drying in the sun, and on the opposite shore a
cram of yachts, cool white except for brasses glistening sun-hot; a waterfront road made frantic
with speeding cars and motorcycles, then rising
upwards from the harbour the houses and hotels,
the shops, the spire and belfries of the capital city,
Mahon, she felt no uplift of spirits, no surge of
warmth in spite of the brilliance of sky and sea,

the hot caress of the sun.

For weeks she had been gripped by an attitude of dazed suspension, a subconscious refusal to admit that the accident had ever hhappened, that the wire attached to a harness designed to 'fly' her high across the stage had not snapped on the closing night of *La Sylphide*, sending her crashing to the stage with one slim, cherished ankle twisted awkwardly beneath her. For the umpteenth time she was reliving the incident that, with the suddenness of a snapping wire, had wrenched from her grasp all hopes of a brilliant career. Top London specialists had exercised all their skill in an effort to restore to her ankle the strength and flexibility built up through years of dedicated training. Exceptional talent is the only currency necessary to gain entry into the ballet world, which was why, with the help of keen-eyed teachers and determined foster-parents, she had been accepted as a pupil by a celebrated ballet school when barely eleven years of age.

The discipline of the ballet world begins young and never ends. Far from being merely pretty entertainers, ballet dancers are forced to train harder than any athlete in any sport, every day of their dancing lives. But because dancing unearthed from within her a lightness of spirit, a happiness almost too great to be borne, and because of the depth of gratitude she had felt towards her foster-parents and the teachers who had been quick to recognise her talent, Birdie had not begrudged one moment of the gruelling exercises designed to bend and stretch a dancer's body into shape, to ensure that balance, control and the correct distribution of body weight are attained. Determined to succeed, she had found the courage to crash her tortured limbs through a barrier of physical pain, and as a consequence, in less than a year she had been judged strong enough to go up on pointe. She had absorbed lessons like a sponge, delighting choreographers with her ability to translate their instructions into fluid movement; gratifying conductors with her perfect sense of timing; amazing teachers with the magically expressive way she was able to convey her feelings without the use of words. No other pupil had taken quite so much to heart the call for dedication, the warnings that even after years of training only a handful of them could hope to reach the top of their profession. She had skipped without regret the lighthearted flirtations and giggling companionship her teenage contemporaries had shared, working at the barre until her muscles had screamed in protest, even forcing back sleep in order to practise in her mind the gestures of mime.

Her reward had come as a solo spot that had brought acclaim from critics and public alike, her future had stretched endless with possibilities, abundant with promise, yet she had felt that a lifetime would barely be long enough to contain all the roles she wished to dance, all the effort she intended to expend in order to reach the pinnacle of perfection. Then, against all odds, in spite of daily checks and painstaking precautions, a flaw in a length of wire had gone undetected . . .

Anthony Ashwell strode soft-footed on deck, his roped-soled shoes giving no warning of his approach. He hesitated at the sight of the girl leaning against the rail, her expression pensive, her body a slim line of dejection which normally, because she was concerned about his self-imposed burden of guilt, he was never allowed to glimpse.

When she shifted slightly, obviously seeking to ease the strain on her injured ankle, he winced. In time, the specialists had promised, the pain would lessen and the limp would become almost imperceptible, but the injury had been so severe that unfortunately a stiffness would always remain—a diagnosis which the majority could accept as a slight inconvenience but which to a budding ballerina had represented crippling disaster. Inevitably, his mind drifted back nine years into the past to the moment when he had first set eyes upon Jennifer Wren, a brown-haired, overawed schoolgirl whose stammered responses to his questions had not impressed him in the least, whose nervous blinking, born, he was later to learn, of a tragically insecure childhood, had irritated him to the point of rudeness. Her combination of muted, almost drab colouring, birdlike timidity, and an unfortunate coupling of names had prompted her fellow pupils to christen her Birdie, but not until she had begun to dance had it become obvious how deserving she was of the unconsciously apt title. The nervous, fluttering girl had responded to the sound of music by spreading her wings and soaring with indescribable grace across the width of the stage. Training had unearthed artistic flair; exercise had developed her exquisite line; maturity had bestowed a pale, haunting beauty and though shyness was inherent she had learnt to hide her feeling behind a mask of serenity, making it difficult to gauge the extent of her hurt, the degree of pain imposed by clipped wings.

As if sensing his presence, she swung round to face him. 'Good morning, Tony!' The warmth of her welcome made nonsense of his theory that she must consider that his negligence had contributed to her accident because as director of the opera company he was ultimately responsible for the safety of every one of its members. 'Don't look so sad,' she read his expression correctly, 'you have been assured over and over again that you were not to blame—it was a mishap no one could have foreseen, an act of God ...' She faltered, then trembled into silence, yearning for sufficient eloquence to rid the sensitive, artistic man of his unjustifiable sense of guilt.

A glint of tears beneath gold-feathered lashes sent him striding towards her, cursing inwardly the self-absorption that had caused her further upset. Determinedly dismissing the subject that caused them both intolerable pain, he hugged her shoulders and confided briskly:

'Daphne is toying with the idea of throwing a party on board this evening. As the yacht is newly commissioned she wishes to show it off to her friends among the yachting fraternity, many of whom she expects to find moored in the harbour when we berth. A *christening* party, would you believe! After much deliberation, our fervent ballet-lover has finally decided upon a name for her new toy. Predictably, she combed the ballet world for a source of inspiration and she's now beaming with complacency at having made what she considers to be a brilliant choice. But please, Birdie, my love, don't ask me what it is . . .'

'Oh, but I must!' she insisted on a gurgling breath. 'You can't keep me in suspense, it would be most unfair!'

'*Terre-à-terre*,' he admitted with a groan. 'If she were anyone other than Lady Daphne Durant, our beloved patroness and balletomane, I would condemn her to the depths of the Mediterranean for her mastery of trite verbiage.'

His fine, rather stern features lightened when a sideways glance confirmed that his deliberately acid observation had succeeded in amusing her. Laughter was bubbling like a well, the pale oval face defined clear as a cameo by dark brown hair, severely parted, then winged to the nape of her neck to nestle in a silken bun; hazel eyes, set within gold-dusted lashes, a sweet, rather solemn mouth that once had been quick to smile, were alive and dancing.

'I don't know about that,' she pretended to consider, struggling to keep the corners of her mouth from lifting. 'I think I'll side with Lady Daphne, I quite like the connotation and consider she's been very clever. *Terre-à-terre*, the ballet term for choreography with few jumps, is a unique name for a yacht, and its literal translation "ground to ground" seems to me to be an excellent choice for a vessel designed to transport people from one land to another.'

'You disappoint me, Birdie,' he groaned. 'I have no alternative but to withdraw from the argument—one illogical female I can fight, but not *two*!'

'You know you think the world of Lady Daphne!' she dared to reprove the man who up until her accident had appeared as aloof and untouchable as some Olympian god, 'so why do you persist in criticising her?'

'Self-defence,' he confessed with wry candour. 'I seldom dare admit even to myself that I adore her.'

'Then why——' she began, then faltered, ashamed of her inquisitiveness.

'. . . don't I ask her to marry me?' he prompted. 'Because she has too much money and because I don't possess sufficient strength of character to rise above the sort of remarks made to men who marry wealthy widows.'

'But you love her,' she protested vehemently, 'and when you're together even a blind person could sense that she's mad about you.'

'Perhaps,' he nodded briefly, his grey eyes clouding, 'but she's also mad about travelling, especially in her own private yacht and accompanied by friends tuned in to her own particular wavelength. Although the majority of her guests are chosen from out of her own aristocratic circle, with a smattering of musicians, painters, literary men, and women famous either for their beauty or their personality, she's by no means a snob— one only needs to be outstanding in some field to be invited on one of her cruises. As you say,' he frowned 'we're in love, yet I keep having to remind myself that we're temperamentally unsuited. Daphne is a nomad, it would be most unfair to expect one of her restless temperament to settle in London for eleven months of every year, in no time at all she would be pining to return to the sun and the idyllic existence she enjoys here in the Mediterranean.'

Birdie parted her lips to argue, then thought better of it. Tony's decision had not been reached lightly, his mind was tortured by doubts, but only Daphne was qualified to convince him that he had drawn a wrong conclusion. So she tried to convey sympathy by leaning her cheek against the slender, sensitive hand resting on her shoulder and murmuring as casually as she was able:

'Poor Lady Daphne, condemned and sentenced without being given the chance to utter one word in self-defence!'

When his grip upon her shoulder tightened she braced to withstand a spate of his notoriously scathing temper, but was spared the ordeal when Lady Daphne's voice intruded, calling him by name.

'Tony! Tony! Oh, there you are,' she trilled appearing from below deck looking anxious and unusually harassed. Sunshine formed a golden nimbus around her hair as she hurried towards them, looking trim and workmanlike in brief denim shorts that displayed to advantage her very shapely legs, and wearing a sleeveless cotton top tucked inside a slim waistband. Conscious always of the need to keep wrinkles at bay, she tried not to frown, but when she reached them the look in her wide blue eyes was doleful.

'I shall have to postpone the party,' she

declared in a tone flat with disappointment.

'Oh ...?' Tony queried warily, familiarity rendering him immune to her dramatic outbursts.

'We've run out of olives,' she confirmed with such an air of tragedy Birdie almost burst out laughing. 'The chef is much too busy to be bothered, and the rest of the crew have been promised time off immediately we dock provided they return in good time to wait upon my guests. So what am I to do?' she wailed. 'There's no one else I can send—unless, Tony darling,' she eyed him speculatively, 'you could run this tiny errand? After all, I shall be busy all day supervising the preparations for tonight, which means that you'll be left at a loose end.'

'Indeed it does not!' he contradicted. 'There are letters I must write and have despatched immediately from Mahon. Besides which,' he sounded slightly irritated, 'if olives are so essential to the success of your party why not postpone it until tomorrow night or even the night after, giving yourself ample time to send out invitations?'

'Invitations!' Lady Daphne drew indignantly erect. 'My dear Tony,' she withered him with a look, 'I *never* need to send out invitations to any of my parties, it's known the length and breadth of the Med that the very first night we drop anchor in any port I'm at home to all friends and acquaintances!'

Sensing a storm brewing between the two volatile personalities, Birdie offered hastily: 'Let me collect the olives, if you'll just head me in the right direction I'll be glad of a chance to stretch my legs.'

'Certainly not,' Tony snapped. 'You can't be allowed to roam about alone in unfamiliar surroundings.'

'Why, thank you, my dear!' Gratefully, Lady Daphne seized upon her offer, allowing Tony's protest to fall upon deaf ears. 'The shop that supplies us with provisions is a mere five minutes' walk from the waterfront, and you're sure to enjoy the stroll. Mahon is a beautiful old town.'

Leaving them locked in heated argument, Birdie slipped down to her cabin to change, then went back on deck, eager to step ashore immediately the yacht had settled into a berth along the stretch of waterfront crammed with yachts of every nation, large and small, ancient and modern, trim and ungainly, battered and sleek, but none that came anywhere near the size and opulence of Lady Daphne's gleaming new toy.

'How nice you look, my dear Birdie!' Lady Daphne beamed, handing over a basket and a slip of paper on which was written the name of the shop and one or two other small items to accompany the olives. 'I've drawn you a map naming each street so that if you should get lost, which is very unlikely, it will be a simple enough matter for you to ask directions, because many Menorquins speak English. Now are you certain you don't mind running this errand?' Belatedly, she looked anxious. 'Tony is so cross with me, he insists that I'm imposing upon your good nature.'

'Nonsense,' Birdie assured her, looking unfamiliar in a green cotton sundress printed with yachts in full sail, narrow at the top where green strings were knotted on each bare shoulder, then billowing like a tent, disguising her slim form completely. A kerchief bound around her head and a pair of huge-rimmed sunglasses ensured her anonymity. 'I'm looking forward to my first foray into foreign territory, also the doctors did emphasise that walking is the best possible exercise for my ankle, remember?'

'Good girl!' her hostess beamed, completely reassured. 'Off you go and enjoy yourself, but promise me that if you feel the least pain in your ankle you'll call a taxi.'

Birdie stepped ashore into an exciting new world, a world filled with noisy vehicles being driven on the wrong side of the road by maniacs with fingers permanently depressing their horns; by smiling faces with merry eyes and skin tanned to shades ranging from nutmeg to darkest ebony; by scantily-clad urchins sitting with legs dangling over the harbour wall dipping home-made fishing lines into crystal blue water alive with tiddlers. Across the width of the road watchful grand-mothers dressed entirely in black sat in the door-ways of humble-looking dwellings, each with a single living-room no bigger than a large boat-house, but with an uninterrupted view of the harbour and beyond that a heavenly blue vista of sea and sky, wheeling gulls, and the sails of fishing boats bringing husbands and sons safely back to harbour.

Inhaling deeply, Birdie picked her way along the waterfront in the direction of the Maritime

Steps she had been told would lead her into town,
trying to identify an assortment of smells, a combination of diesel oil, shellfish, strong cheese and
spiced sausages, the perfume of orange trees and
flowering shrubs running riot over the hillside
propping up the town, then lastly, the intoxicating
odour coming from a gin distillery she had been
surprised to discover tucked in between a work-
man's café and a shop selling local handicrafts.

At the top of the steps she stopped to consult
her map, then set off in the direction indicated to
find the shop that supplied their provisions. She
took her time, sauntering along streets so narrow
pedestrians had to turn sideways on the foot-wide
pavements to avoid cars brushing past. Revelling
in the breeze that turned a network of alleyways
into cool, whitewashed wind tunnels, she stole
glances through open doorways and saw sparsely
furnished but spotlessly clean kitchens where tiles
and dishes sparkled and a pan of soup seemed to
be simmering on every stove.

'If you prefer, we could deliver these goods to
Lady Daphne's yacht,' the proprietress assured
her in hesitant English when eventually Birdie
found the small general store so choc-à-bloc with
goods she had to tread a careful path towards the
counter.

'Thank you, but as they weigh so little I'll take
them with me,' she declined politely, suppressing
a smile at the sight of a notice hung prominently
on one wall, misprinted in English, 'We deliver
slopping to your yacht'.

'I'll have a pound of plums, please.' She indicated a mound of luscious-looking fruit, each one three times the size of any she had seen at home.

Sticky juice ran down her chin when she succumbed to the temptation of sampling one while, with the basket dangling over her arm, she continued on her way, drawn to explore the sights and sounds of activity issuing from the far end of the narrow thoroughfare. With a feeling of pleasurable guilt she demolished the whole of the purple, sun-sweetened fruit, savouring its delicious flavour but guiltily aware that, in spite of natural slimness, she would not have dared to indulge in such luxury while still in training.

Her mind was far away when she stepped off the kerb to avoid a toddler playing on the pavement outside his home. A screech of brakes was her first intimation of danger, then as she swung round, startled, to discover a chromium-plated bumper bar brushing her skirt, a string of Spanish imprecations became audible from the interior of a sleek white limousine. Shock held her rigid as a man climbed from behind the wheel and strode furiously towards her.

'*Idiota! Imbécil!*' She had no difficulty interpreting the meaning of those two words, although the rest of his angrily-snapped tirade was beyond her. Staring with mouth agape, her basket swinging limply, and with plum juice staining her chin, she must have fitted beautifully the role he had allocated with such certainty. Several times the word *muchacha* was hurled above her startled head before impatient hands gripped her by the waist to lift her bodily on to the pavement.

As he strode back to his car she heard a child's thin treble piping a question from the depths of the capacious rear seat.

'*Un poco loco!*' he responded, tapping his head with a meaningful gesture and casting Birdie a look of withering scorn. A peal of childish laughter was interpretation enough. Indignation jerked her from her shocked trance, but even as she started towards the car, intending to give the arrogant Spaniard a piece of her mind, she heard the soft kiss of tyres against cobbles, then felt a whoosh of warm air as the glittering white monster drove off, leaving her shaking with anger, feeling scorched by the wake of a fiery dragon.

CHAPTER TWO

THE chef had been instructed to prepare a cold buffet for a limitless number of people.

They began arriving as soon as darkness fell, starting as a dribble of twos and threes, then developing into a continuous stream until the gangplank seemed permanently crammed and an overspill of guests had to be accommodated on neighbouring yachts that were packed so tightly into the harbour it was possible for the young and active to manoeuvre from deck to deck. An international regatta was due to begin the following day, which probably explained, Birdie thought, why every yacht that had ever been built seemed to have sailed into Mahon harbour, their owners all intimately acquainted with Lady Daphne.

Champagne corks were popping, toasts were being proposed for the happy cruises of the newly-christened *Terre-à-terre*, when she decided that the party had reached a stage where she would not be missed. She began making her way to her cabin, feeling strangely out of tune with the crush of exhilarated guests, the jarring sound of modern hit records drifting on the breeze, the reflection of tiny lights casting a harsh diamanté stole over the black velvet sea. Her near-accident earlier that day had left her feeling strangely jumpy, as nervy and tense as if she were awaiting her cue to appear on stage at the beginning of an important opening night. The image of the impatient Spaniard had refused to fade from her mind; the grip of his fingers seemed permanently imprinted upon her waist; his ill-tempered sarcasm still resounded in her ears in spite of the babble of conversation, the raucous blare of music.

Birdie had almost reached her goal when a hand clutched her elbow and Lady Daphne's frantic voice wailed in her ear.

'Birdie, why do I do it? I've got to have people with me when I'm at sea, otherwise life would become such a bore, but I never expected such a stampede of guests, my staff can't cope! I'm having to help out myself—would you be a darling and lend a hand?'

She hesitated, casting a dubious glance at her one and only evening gown, a starkly simple black jersey with scooped-out neckline and tiny cap sleeves, but after a quick mental scolding, she hastened to agree:

'Of course, I should be glad to.'

Lady Daphne gaily insisted upon entering into the spirit of things by ferreting out a couple of aprons. Her own looked incongruous worn over an apricot silk dress, but the effect made by dainty white muslin against Birdie's black dress was startling.

Lady Daphne clapped her hands and exclaimed with delighted amusement. 'Ah, si! Tony has often commented upon your genius for adapting to any part you're called upon to play, and he's so right! Simply by donning an apron you've been transformed into a perfect *muchacha*, a demure little servant girl.'

So that was what he had labelled her! As she circulated the throng with trays of drinks, looking outwardly composed but inwardly seething, Birdie was rehearsing in her mind what she would have liked to have said to the man who had harangued her as he would a servant, no doubt ordering her to stop wasting her employer's time by dawdling in the streets!

Obviously her outfit must have helped to foster the illusion. Many of the young Spanish girls she had seen had been wearing modern dress, most had had kerchiefs binding their hair, and some had even worn sunglasses.

She thought her mind was playing her tricks when, projecting from somewhere behind her shoulder, she heard once again the precisely pronounced, arrogantly assured voice, speaking in English this time, but still unmistakably *his*! Slowly she turned in the direction of the sound, and immediately her fear was confirmed. His companion was very young, very lovely, and obviously very impressed by the Spaniard who would not have looked out of place in the company of dark-turbanned Moors clattering through narrow streets, hawk on wrist, riding to the hunt, or standing on the quarterdeck of a great Spanish galleon, eager for battle. The puzzling colour of his eyes—deep Saxon blue against dark tan—was explained when unashamedly she eavesdropped upon their conversation and heard his dry, slightly bored reply to a previous remark the girl had made.

'No, it would not be entirely true to say that we Menorquins dislike the English, but I must admit to the existence of a certain animosity. Because many of my race have inherited the characteristics of Moorish settlers, almost Nordic in appearance, we are often accused of possessing English blood. In some cases this is possible—though not in my own—because at one time, *señorita*, England was an occupying power in our island. Centuries ago English artillery battered our defences until, in order to avoid more unnecessary carnage, we were forced to surrender. But the blood that was shed will never be forgotten. As part of our history, the story of our occupation will be passed on from generation to generation.'

The girl had hung on to his every word, yet it was obvious, to Birdie at least, that her main interest was not the past but in the very exciting present. Casting him a look so flirtatious Birdie cringed, she sighed the outrageous admission.

'I do hope that English *women* meet with your approval, Conde, for we're all agreed that Spanish men are exceptionally good-looking and experts at making love.'

For the first time in her life Birdie felt an uge to act violently against a member of her own sex. The fact that the girl was young and obviously bowled over by the Spaniard's good looks was no excuse for forgetting that she was now in a country where high moral standards were still the accepted norm, a country whose women, though not physically cloistered, were as morally imprisoned as in the days when they saw the world only through the fretted screens of their windows. She winced for the reputation of all English girls, was even moved to feel pity for the girl who had aroused his distaste, when the Conde's cold, distant reply began to register.

'Unfortunately, *señorita*, our young men are vain enough to react to such flattery with all the ardour they once applied to acquiring knowledge of fishing and navigation. These days, thanks to shoals of liberated females in search of amorous adventures, our fishing profession is losing all its men, for the youngsters have discovered newer and more amusing ways of earning a living. And now, if you will excuse me, *señorita*, I must leave.' Stiffly he bowed, his expression cold as the ice clinking in his glass. 'I promised my family that my absence would be a short one, that I would be away only long enough to pay my respects to Lady Daphne.'

He lifted his head, obviously searching, and to Birdie's horror began making straight towards her. Her fingers clenched around the rim of her tray, using it as a support to steady her trembling hands, as a shield between herself and the advancing foe. But his glance was impersonal when he stopped to deposit his glass upon her empty tray, his muttered '*Gracias*' almost inaudible as he passed on his way, leaving her feeling, for the second time that day, reduced to the ranks of a serving wench.

It was early morning by the time the last of the guests had made their reluctant departure. Thankfully, Birdie disposed of her apron and headed towards her cabin, feeling tired enough to sleep the clock round, yet with nerves set indefinably on edge. Lady Daphne, however, delayed her with a request. She was too animated for sleep, eager to hold an inquest on the party, to comment on the presence of her many influential and distinguished friends.

'Do join Tony and me in a nightcap before retiring, Birdie dear.'

'Oh, but . . .' She searched her weary mind for an excuse.

'Just five minutes more,' Lady Daphne coaxed. 'I'm far too excited to sleep. I would have preferred the party to go on until dawn, but as many of my guests are due to take part in the regatta I dared not suggest it. It went well, don't you think?' She sparkled at Tony, propelling Birdie towards a couch. 'They all seemed to be having an enjoyable evening.'

'You're fishing for compliments,' he chided with a grin, slipping a fond arm around her shoulders. 'You're perfectly well aware that as you're the acknowledged queen of society hostesses your parties are always successful. Although, come to think of it, there was one chap who proved to be an exception, he seemed in quite a hurry to get away.'

'Oh, who . . .?' Lady Daphne looked aggrieved.

'Don't know his name,' Tony shrugged, reaching for a cigarette, 'he left before we were introduced, but I took him to be a Spaniard, a tall, dark guy who would look perfect cast in the role of El Cid.'

Birdie tensed, suddenly wide awake. Only one man present at the party had merited comparison with the Spanish hero whose exploits, real and legendary, had inspired tales of romance and tragedy.

Lady Daphne was quick to recognise the connection. 'Oh, you mean Vulcan—Conde de la Conquista de Retz, to give him his proper title—yes, he did leave early, but it was sweet of him to come at all, considering the pressures upon his time.'

Birdie remained silent, mentally clamouring for Lady Daphne to elaborate, secretly shocked by an urgent longing to know more about the man who made her feel insignificant as a servant in the presence of a lord.

Much to her relief, Tony proved to be equally curious.

'Pressure is a hazard one must learn to accept in today's cut-throat society,' he stated mildly, 'a burden everyone has to tolerate.'

'I was not referring to that type of pressure,' she corrected swiftly. 'Vulcan has interests in many successful companies both in Menorca and on the Spanish mainland, nevertheless, I can't imagine him bending under the strain of business, he's too much of a fighter not to enjoy a challenge. As you so cleverly implied, my intuitive darling, Vulcan is a modern-day El Cid who uses boardroom battles as a substitute for slaying Moors. But his stress is emotional, he's manacled by a strict sense of duty, by a determination to fulfil what he considers to be his sole obligation.'

'A contradictory statement to make about a man you've just likened to the ruthless El Cid,' Tony murmured.

'It must seem so,' she smiled agreement, 'but if ever you're privileged to know the Spanish people well, you'll realise that their emotional temperament leads them to extremes which may seem false and contradictory to strangers who don't understand them.'

Birdie blessed Tony for being tuned in to her own wavelength when he let the comment pass with a nod and prodded further.

'Obviously some female has our Spanish friend in her clutches—a compelling, dark-eyed *señorita*, no doubt?'

Fleetingly, Birdie wondered why Lady Daphne's nod should cause her heart to plummet.

'Yes, you're right, a jealous, possessive little minx who's all of five years old.'

Even the mildly interested Tony was startled to attention. '*Five* years old, you say . . .?'

Lady Daphne laughed, pleased with the stir she had caused. 'Vulcan is not a man to discuss intimate family affairs, but rumour has it that the child, Lucita, is the daughter of a distant cousin with whom he was very much in love, and continued to love even after she married someone else. Lucita was just a baby when her parents lost their lives in a boating accident, and as neither of them had any close relatives, Vulcan, being the sort of man he is, immediately assumed responsibility for the child. Then about two years ago,' she sighed, 'as if that were not sufficient tragedy in any young life, Lucita contracted polio, a slight attack from which she recovered well except for a deformity of one foot which, as there's been no recent sign of improvement, one must assume will affect her for the rest of her life.'

When Tony made no attempt to broach the next logical question, Birdie asked:

'What about the Conde's wife, doesn't she help out with the child?'

'He has no wife, Lucita has seen to that. Many lovely girls, all aspiring to the title of Condesa de Retz, have entered Vulcan's life and then been immediately ousted, vetoed by an autocratic infant determined to keep him to herself.'

'Then he can't have been in love with any of them,' Tony snorted. 'No man worth his salt would allow any obstacle to stand between himself and the woman he wanted to marry.'

He realised that he had fallen into a trap of his own making when her reply came, sweetly iced. 'My own sentiments exactly, Tony darling! Isn't it amazing how quickly we can spot in others failings that we refuse to acknowledge in ourselves?' Smothering a yawn, she rose to her feet. 'Which reminds me, I've invited Vulcan and Lucita to tea tomorrow—today,' she amended, 'and if I'm to retain my reputation as a perfect hostess I must try to get some sleep.'

After hours of tossing restlessly in her bed, Birdie was forced to come to terms with the fact that ironically, she and Lady Daphne had swapped roles. Eventually, when daybreak dawned, she abandoned all thought of sleep, consoling herself with the fact that her pale face and shadowed eyes were immaterial because she intended to abscond, to absent herself from the yacht until she was certain that the danger of having to pass around tea and scones and of making polite conversation with the intimidating Conde was well past.

She sauntered into breakfast dressed in the uniform of the sun-worshipper, skimpy shorts pulled on over a swimsuit; a loose camisole top, flat sandals, and carrying a wide-brimmed straw hat and beachbag containing towels, purse, suntan lotion and a jar of after-sun cream.

Tony was sipping coffee, Lady Daphne was toying with a minute portion of scrambled egg, but both looked up, registering surprise at her appearance.

'Are you going somewhere special?' Tony sounded slightly accusing.

'I thought I'd take a bus down to the nearest beach,' Birdie replied brightly, helping herself to toast and marmalade. 'Last night I was given directions to the nearest bus depot and assured that there's a regular shuttle service from the town to the beach every half hour. As I'll probably be away for most of the day,' she apologised to Lady Daphne, 'I hope you don't mind my having asked the chef to let me have a packed lunch to take with me?'

'Of course I don't mind,' Lady Daphne assured her politely, 'but what a shame you'll miss meeting the Conde de Retz—he too is a lover of the ballet and also a very interesting conversationalist.'

'I'm sorry too,' Birdie trained all her attention on the piece of toast she was buttering, almost choking on the lie, 'but as he's such an old friend you're bound to have lots to talk about, so I thought my presence would be superfluous.'

'And what about me?' Tony sounded indignant.

'I don't fancy playing gooseberry while Daphne lavishes attention upon her Spanish conde!'

Birdie's face was a picture of indecision when Lady Daphne came to her rescue. 'I make only one strict rule for my guests, Tony dear, and that is that they must spend their time exactly as they wish. And besides that,' a dimple flashed in her cheek, 'with young Lucita to keep you company, I can safely promise that you won't be bored.'

A long queue had formed by the time Birdie arrived at the bus depot, tourists mostly, whose pale complexions, perspiring faces and fractious children labelled them fairly recent arrivals. The din and the heat inside the bus once they were all crammed inside was unbearable. Squashed into a rear corner seat with a fat woman's elbow digging into her ribs and sunshine dazzling through glass with the precison of a laser beam, Birdie found her thoughts winging with envy back to the yacht where Tony and Lady Daphne would by now be stretched out beneath a shady awning with an ice-cool drink near to hand, gaining maximum benefit from the offshore breeze that continually teased around the perimeter of the island.

'It's your own stupid fault!' mentally she scolded herself, gritting her teeth as the bus jolted over rough, unsurfaced roads leading to the south of the island. Rivulets of sweat were trickling between her shoulderblades, the atmosphere inside the bus had the damp humidity of a Turkish bath, by the time it jerked to a halt to allow its gasping passengers to escape on to a dusty, sunbaked car park.

But just a few hundred yards away lay a flat blue strip of sea. Uttering whoops of delight, the children began racing towards it, floundering ankle-deep in soft white sand, but struggling onwards, their gazes fixed as if fearing their goal might turn out to be a mirage.

Birdie hesitated only long enough to attract the attention of a man in charge of sun-loungers and beach umbrellas, then, once she had staked her claim to a minute portion of the crowded beach, she stripped off her shorts and top and ran down to the breakers to bask blissfully in the shallows.

She had finished her lunch and was stretched out in the sun to dry when sounds of unusual activity jerked her upright. The entire beach population seemed to be on the move, shaking sand out of towels, packing items of picnicware, gathering up toys and a miscellany of articles scattered all around. She just had time to register that the sky had darkened when the first raindrops splashed, large as coins, upon her bare shoulders. Hastily she scrambled to her feet, intent upon following the example of the crowd, but she had left it too late; the heavens parted and a deluge rained from the sky, soaking in seconds the shorts and top she had left lying on the sand, plastering her swimsuit to her limbs and lending a seal-dark sleekness to her head.

The misery of her fellow passengers was evident when they were disgorged from the bus into rain-swept Mahon. More damp and uncomfortable than she had ever been in her life before, Birdie plodded doggedly in the direction of the

CHAPTER THREE

WHEN Birdie returned to the salon, dried off and respectably attired in a brown cotton dress as inconspicuous as the plumage of the timid bird after which she had been named, she saw at a glance that the Conde de la Conquista de Retz was not amused.

Tony had regained his equilibrium; Lady Daphne's mouth kept teasing upwards in an amused smile; Lucita, an enchantingly mature child whose piquant features, dark eyes and rioting black curls held a promise of great beauty, erupted into giggles each time she glanced at Birdie who, after scurrying into a seat in a corner, began crumbling the cake on her plate between agitated fingers, trying to subdue the blush that had scorched her cheeks from the moment the Conde had released her and stepped back to apologise with chilling disdain:

'Forgive me, *señorita*, I must remember in future never to condemn a nut because of the state of its shell.'

If only I were a nut, she was thinking miserably, *with a shell to hide me from eyes of blue flint that spark annoyance whenever he's forced to look at me!*

His young ward, however, was registering unqualified approval. Obviously spoiled and pampered, isolated from children of her own age because of her illness, she had spent her entire life in the company of adults whose attitudes she found boringly predictable. But towards Birdie she displayed an immediate affinity—she too had cringed from the lash of his scolding tongue, she too had suffered the humiliation of being hauled into the presence of adults to account for some trifling misdemeanour, but the most gratifying discovery of all was the fact that, in a world that seemed full of physically perfect people, there was one in addition to herself who was also lame.

'Señorita Birdie . . .!' The plate almost jerked out of Birdie's grasp when the childish yet self-assured voice demanded her attention. 'Why are you named after a bird?'

'Don't be impertinent, Lucita!' The Conde's tone rang cool with displeasure.

'But, Tio, *I* should like to take the name of a bird!' she protested, quite undeterred by his sharp warning glance. Birdie tensed, anticipating a look that would reduce the child to silence, only to be confounded when she saw his lips twitch with amusement, his hard glance soften as it rested fondly upon his precocious ward.

'Very well, my little parrot, you shall be,' he teased with a gentleness that left Birdie mentally floundering.

'No, *no*, Tio . . .!' Lucita giggled a delighted protest. 'I want a name similar to Señorita Birdie's so that perhaps I might grow up to walk grace-fully, to seem to float on air as she does, in spite of being lame!'

A heartfelt silence fell, a silence filled with sympathy for the beautiful child so sensitive to her disability. Even the Conde looked so helpless Tony felt moved to intervene. Clearing a huskiness from his throat, he began explaining quietly:

'A boy does not grow big simply because he has been given a giant's name, Lucita, but rather the reverse. If a boy should develop the characteristics of a giant and suddenly begin to grow tall then his friends will quickly note the comparison and re-christen him with an appropriate name. That was the way it happened with Birdie ...' Birdie's embarrassment became acute when every head turned in her direction. '... She was not born graceful, with a step as light as thistledown; the carriage you envy was achieved by years of training, hard exercise, and dedication of the mind. As a child, she was christened Birdie by her fellow pupils because she was apt to flutter with a shyness that made her appear awkward, ungainly as a cygnet who had not gained proper use of its legs, but once she was taught how to dance the cygnet turned into a swan, a graceful ballerina whose spectacular leaps and acrobatic feats of ballet enraptured audiences all over the world.'

Feeling the Conde's speculative glance upon her ankle, Birdie blushed crimson and thrust it out of sight beneath her chair, annoyed with Tony Tony for reviving memories she would have preferred to forget, and for forcing a man to revise his opinion of a girl he had twice treated as a servant and once, unbelievably, as a common thief. She could almost sense the questions forming on his lips, but was spared his inquisition when Lucita uttered a cry of wonder and slid from her chair to limp across the carpet until she was near enough to rest small, pleading hands upon her knee.

'Please, *señorita*,' she gulped, her wide brown eyes fastened upon Birdie's face, 'could you show *me* how to become as graceful as a swan? With you to teach me I *know* I could dance!'

'Oh, of course you could, darling!' Aching with compassion, Birdie clasped the child in a warm, encouraging hug.

Abruptly, the Conde rose to his feet. 'That's enough, Lucita, it is time for us to go!'

'But, Tio . . .!' she wailed.

'No argument, if you please,' he snapped icily.

For a second Lucita stared into his implacable face, her body tense, fists bunched with impotent rage, then suddenly, employing the guile of a woman four times her age, she flashed him a sweet smile.

'Very well, Tio,' she capitulated demurely, limping forward to place a small, trusting hand in his.

Lady Daphne turned aside when she read his expression of startled relief, her quirk of amusement broadening to a wide grin when she caught Birdie's eye and realised that she, too, had seen through the young charmer's ploy. Bringing great effort to bear, they managed to keep their faces straight until the Conde was out of earshot, but once his car had disappeared from view they startled Tony by dissolving into uncontrollable laughter.

'What's so funny?' he appealed. 'Am I to be allowed to share the joke?'

'Oh, dear!' gasped Lady Daphne, holding her aching sides, 'is it any wonder that men are so often deceived when their insight into the ways of women extends no farther than the ends of their noses?'

'I haven't the faintest idea what you're talking about,' Tony retorted, completely bewildered.

'I believe you,' Lady Daphne gurgled, sinking down into a convenient chair, 'nor has poor Vulcan the slightest idea that he's about to be hoodwinked by the child who I suspect is a reincarnation of Eve! How could anyone be blind to such guile?' she appealed to Birdie. 'I should make a deal with her, if I were you,' she twinkled. 'When she returns—as she most certainly will once Vulcan has been brought to heel—I should offer to teach her to dance on condition that she shares with you the secret of her ability to lull a man's suspicions, to outwit even the hawk-eyed Vulcan, without his having the faintest notion that he's being manipulated.'

'My dear Daphne,' Tony drawled rebuke, 'you speak like a novice who imagines that the art of dancing can be taught in minutes. Need I remind you that we're due back in London at the end of the month?'

'*You* are, Tony dear,' she mused thoughtfully, 'but I can think of no reason why Birdie should not take advantage of an opportunity to revel in sunshine for a month or two, to give herself time to recuperate from her accident and to sort out in her mind what she intends to do with the rest of her life.'

Birdie's heart lurched when the problem she had deliberately pushed to the back of her mind was suddenly brought out into the open. Sensitive to her distress, Tony leapt in with the assurance:

'Though Birdie's ankle will not permit her to dance strenuous roles, she still has much to contribute to the ballet world,' he reminded Daphne coldly. 'Her knowledge and expertise will make her invaluable as a teacher and she will also be called upon to play the occasional mime role.'

His words lifted the blanket of depression from Birdie's spirits. To be allowed to play an immobile part in the steady flow of organised movement that made up a ballet, to mime to music instead of participating with skilful body movement designed to move audiences to laughter or tears, would be bread without jam, egg without salt, but at least it would prevent her from being starved of contact with the ballet world. Acting without words, conveying feelings without the use of speech, was a vital part of the ballet; there were movements that demanded a set of gestures to put across the story, gestures that were a part of the sign language of mime understood all over the world. Undoubtedly, she would find immobile roles frustrating, nevertheless she had been trained to convey joy when her heart was breaking, to express laughter when her throat was aching with the throb of unshed tears. In her final role she had been cast as a sylph, an elemental being that inhabited the air, an insubstantial presence hovering between the choice of living in the physical or the spiritual world, but with her fall to earth the decision had ceased to be hers—there was no choice of role in the world of fantasy for a human cripple!

Filled with an overwhelming sense of gratitude, she gulped, 'Thank you, Tony. I wish I could bring myself to refuse your offer, but I know I possess neither the courage nor the will to train for any other career. The world of ballet is the only world I know, to be cut off from it would be comparable to being deprived of a limb. I know that at first it will be hard to accustom myself to being more or less a bystander,' her throat closed tight as a vice, 'but I'm willing to undertake any task, however menial, in order to stay with the company.'

'Birdie, my dear,' Lady Daphne's voice was not quite steady, 'are you sure you've come to the right decision? I can understand your reluctance to make a clean break, but I wish you would give yourself more time to think about your future. Why not consider my previous suggestion?' she urged with rising enthusiasm. 'A long procession of ladies—governesses, tutors, companions, call them what you will—has passed beneath the portals of the Casa de Solitario and been quickly turfed out again. Vulcan has despaired of ever finding a suitable companion for his wayward ward, therefore if you should be offered the post—and I don't doubt that Lucita is at this very moment exercising all her wiles towards that end—you would be doing both yourself and Vulcan a favour by accepting.'

Birdie had placed so little importance upon Lady Daphne's prediction that she was thrown into utter confusion when the very next morning a servant delivered to the yacht a letter inviting Lady Daphne, Tony and herself to the Conde's residence that afternoon to take tea.

'Oh, what a pity!' Lady Daphne exclaimed with suspicious alacrity. 'Tony and I have a previous engagement, but you must go, Birdie, and convey our apologies to the Conde in person.'

'No, I couldn't . . .!' she protested, appalled at the idea of being forced into what amounted to solitary confinement with the intimidating Conde.

'But you must!' Lady Daphne was already scribbling a note of acceptance on her behalf. 'Lucita has obviously worked hard upon her uncle, and now that her spell has worked she'll be terribly disappointed if you should fail to appear. There!' with a sigh of satisfaction she sealed the note in an envelope and passed it to the waiting manservant. 'The deed is done, you *can't* back out now.'

Half an hour before the Conde's limousine was due to pick her up, Birdie was ready and waiting, prowling the deserted deck, her quick, nervous steps marking time with agitated thoughts. Would he be his usual forbidding self, or would breeding demand a show of politeness towards even an unwanted guest? Yet breeding had not managed to disguise his resentment at being made to look a fool. Once the misunderstanding had been sorted out, his manner towards her had been so impeccably polite that only she had been uncomfortably aware of the crystal-blue stare betraying a stirring of the deep-rooted animosity Menorquins had nurtured for centuries against their English foes.

By the time the chauffeur-driven limousine

arrived she had worked herself into a state of acute anxiety. Mentally indicting Lady Daphne for her well-meaning interference, she made her way down the gangplank, but with nerves so shaken she stumbled and almost fell into the opulent embrace of a suede-upholstered seat so spacious that when the car moved off she fell back floundering.

In no time at all, or so it seemed, via a succession of narrow streets and busy thoroughfares, the car drew to a standstill in a quiet secluded alleyway in front of a pair of wrought iron gates through which she glimpsed a patio lined with tubs filled with flowers splashing brilliant daubs of colour against whitewashed walls; a marble fountain spouting water through the lips of a pouting cherub, and a flight of stone steps leading up to a solid, heavily carved door.

With a muttered apology the chauffeur stepped in front of her to tug once on an iron bellpull, then stepped aside when almost immediately the door was opened by a middle-aged woman dressed in severe black with a bunch of keys hanging from the belt around her waist, in the manner of a dignified chatelaine.

'Please come this way,' she instructed Birdie without a trace of a smile disturbing her thin lips. 'El Conde is expecting you.'

With her heels tapping erratically as her heart-beats, Birdie followed in the woman's wake across a marble floor, then through a doorway into a room lined from floor to ceiling with shelves full of books.

'The Señorita Wren has arrived, *señor*,' the

woman announced, then quietly withdrew, leaving her staring across a long stretch of carpet at the tall figure standing directly in the path of sunshine filtering through fine net curtains, still and expressionless as an image on a stained-glass window.

'*Buenas tardes*, Señorita Wren, please take a seat.'

'*Gracias*,' she mumbled, conscious of being scrutinised closely as a butterfly on a pin as she limped towards a chair. He had indicated a comfortable armchair, but she made the mistake of choosing instead a strictly functional straight-backed chair placed directly in front of his desk which, immediately she sat down, transported her back to her schooldays and the few occasions when she had been called to appear before her headmistress for a reprimand. Steadying shaking fingers around the clasp of her handbag, she managed to husk:

'Lady Daphne and Tony asked me to convey regrets for their absence; they had already made arrangements to meet friends before your invitation arrived.'

'I know.' The cool admission left her breathless. 'I was there when the appointment was made, which is why I chose this particular time; I wanted to speak to you alone.' His severe expression did not soften as he sat down opposite and began regarding her coldly across the width of the desk.

'Oh, I see . . .' she gasped, then floundered, wondering what on earth he had to say to her that was so important it needed to be said in private.

'But first of all,' he continued without warmth, 'may I say how sorry I was to learn of the accident that put an end to what I believe was a very promising career.'

Birdie winced from the pain of discovering herself to have been an object of discussion, then jerked to attention when he added, 'When one has dedicated one's life to a career it must be difficult to be suddenly cast adrift, talents rendered useless, and with no other option but to seek a niche in the outside world. Nevertheless,' his tone developed an even harder edge, 'though your situation may be desperate, it does not justify the cruelty of encouraging a crippled child to believe herself capable of being taught to dance simply in order to manoeuvre yourself into suitable employment.'

Her dazed brown eyes roved his face, seeking the meaning behind his outrageous words. 'I don't understand . . .' she faltered, then gasped into silence when his knuckles gleamed white around the hilt of a paper-knife before thrusting downward, jabbing through a blotter with terrifying force.

'How very predictable!' he sneered, jerking to his feet to stride angrily towards the window where, keeping his back turned towards her, he fought to regain control of his temper.

His voice, when he continued speaking, held a note of calmness totally at variance with a man who seemed to have inherited all the qualities of his namesake—Vulcan, god of fire. Consequently it sounded all the more frightening. 'Because you were once successful in making me look a fool,

Señorita Wren, do not be foolhardy enough to attempt to repeat that small triumph. You may have managed to bewitch my young ward into believing that your show of compassion hides no ulterior motive, but she is, as yet, too young to appreciate the damage done to our people in the past by the acquisitive English, or to understand the more insidious danger of moral contagion being imposed upon our youth by an invasion of your permissive-minded contemporaries. I suspect,' he concluded disdainfully, 'that England is a paradise filled with angels of cant, hypocrisy and immorality!'

Until called upon to defend her country, Birdie had not imagined herself to be wildly patriotic, but his derogatory condemnation unearthed feelings she had not known she possessed, a resentment of unjust criticism that drove her to her feet, flaring:

'Even if that were true, which it certainly is not, such a paradise would be preferable to a hell inhabited by narrow-minded bigots! Also, *señor*, I should point out that the penalty for harbouring a spirit of general distrust is that very often the suspicious mind turns hypothesis into fact.'

When he swung round to face her she slumped back into her chair, cowed by a combination of her own temerity and his glacial, narrow-eyed stare.

'Are you implying that I am exaggerating the effect of your influence upon my ward? That to allow you to raise her hopes of becoming a proficient dancer would not inflict a mental distress far greater than the pain she has already suffered

physically? The child is besotted with the notion
of becoming a dancer, she has thought of nothing
else, talked of nothing else, since yesterday when
you so irresponsibly encouraged her to believe
that every lame duck can be transformed into a
swan! Tell me, señorita,' he hissed hatefully, 'if it
is so easy for a cripple to be healed, why aren't
you now practising at the barre instead of angling
so desperately for a job?'

Birdie whitened at the taunt, her eyes blank as
the windows of an empty house as she fought to
overcome the agony of regret that overwhelmed
her each time she was brought face to face with
the reality of an empty future. But she had been
too well schooled in the art of hiding her feelings
to allow him the satisfaction of knowing that this
thrust had plunged deep. Though every nerve in
her body felt stretched, she managed to keep her
voice cool as spring water on a blazing day.

'I do not profess to be a miracle worker, *señor*,
nevertheless, I do believe that Lucita could be
helped by the sort of exercises dancers practise in
order to add flexibility and strength to ankles and
feet. However,' she rose from her chair in one
smooth, graceful movement, 'an opinion is all I'm
prepared to offer, for contrary to your belief I am
not desperate for employment, and even if I were,
as a prospective employer you would not match
up to my requirements.'

She heard his hiss of disbelief as she walked
towards the door and one tiny, arrogant English
part of her rejoiced in the knowledge that never
before had El Conde de la Conquista de Retz been
so thoroughly snubbed.

Affront echoed in his voice when, just as she reached the door, he ordered: 'Wait! I have not yet finished!'

Controlling an inner quaking, she turned enquiring eyes towards him.

'I should like your assurance,' he glinted, 'that should there be any further meeting between yourself and Lucita, you will convey to her as explicitly as you have just conveyed to me that you are totally uninterested in her welfare.'

'I couldn't lie,' she refused gently. 'I feel a great pity for your ward and would very much like——'

'Pity . . .!' The incredulous word sounded foreign on his proud tongue. 'You feel *pity* for a child who has been cosseted from birth, who has everything she could possibly wish for?'

'I'm afraid so,' she nodded gravely, 'you see, *señor*, I feel able to identify with Lucita not only because we share the same physical disability but because I too know what it's like to be an orphan. Granted, I grew up in an environment starved of luxuries, but it was a hundred times blessed with contentment and love.'

For a moment he stared long and hard, then seemed to force himself to question stiffly: 'Does Lucita give the impression that she is not loved?'

She strove for diplomacy. 'You admitted to being excessively indulgent, did you not, *señor*? Ask yourself honestly, is your indulgence an excuse for *self*-indulgence? Are the gifts you heap upon the child a substitute for listening time? Wardrobes full of dresses are useless if there's no audience to admire them. To be lenient towards an unruly child is the easy way out but, strangely, a child uses discipline as a measure of affection and would choose to weather the smack of a caring hand rather than to be passed over unnoticed.'

She let herself out of the house, moving quietly across the hall in case she should attract the attention of the dragon in black who had allowed her admittance, trembling in the aftermath of her own daring, slightly worried about leaving El Conde de la Conquista de Retz looking confounded, too stunned even to notice her exit.

CHAPTER FOUR

BIRDIE had been walking for less than five minutes when at the end of a narrow street she erupted into the town's main square and found it alive with people scurrying from shop to shop, darting across narrow streets, dodging lines of hooting traffic, and strolling leisurely through a pedestrian precinct lined with fabulous boutiques, jewellers, needlework shops displaying samples of Menorquin handicraft, shops crammed with elegant shoes and boots fashioned from soft leather and supple suede for which the island was renowned, together with plaited belts, gorgeous handbags and cosy sheepskin slippers so inexpensive they were piled in every convenient corners, reduced to the level of a contemptuous afterthought.

Her interview with the Conde had left her with a dry throat, so, spotting a vacant seat amid a sea of tables set in the centre of the square, she made a beeline towards it and sat down, thankful for the shade cast by an immense tree whose branches were spreading a leafy roof over the outdoor café.

'*Una copa de limón, por favour,*' she stumbled, smiling shyly at the waiter who had hastened across to serve her. The lemon juice, freshly squeezed over a base of cracked ice, topped up with water, then flavoured with sugar, tasted tart-sweet and refreshingly cool. Slowly she sipped, savouring with her tongue the tangy flavour of lemon, savouring with her eyes the colourful, bustling scene, and eavesdropping unashamedly upon the rapid, unintelligible conversation taking place between two young sailors at an adjoining table.

Her absorption was so complete that when a voice addressed her by name she looked up, her expression dazed, as she stared at the proud, dark head lowering towards her.

'May I be permitted to join you, *señorita*?'

When the request was repeated she blushed and nodded hastily, alarmed by the frown hovering between black winged brows. '*Gracias*.' The Conde looked relieved when he sat down beside her. 'I thought for a moment you had found my lapse of manners unforgivable. The swiftness of your departure caught me unawares—for the past half hour I have been searching the streets hoping to be given an opportunity to apologise and to make up for my lack of courtesy.'

'Apologise for what . . .?' She swallowed hard, her throat once more suddenly dry.

'For allowing you to leave my house without an escort,' he told her gravely, his eyes no longer sparking anger. 'Also I did ask you to have tea with me, remember?'

Finding his show of friendliness even more disconcerting than his dislike, she trembled a laugh.

'You had no need to be worried about me, *señor*, I'm quite used to wandering about on my own.'

'Then you ought not to be,' he replied sharply. 'Without fear of contradiction I can claim that a woman alone can walk without fear among my own countrymen, but you would be wise to bear

in mind the fact that during the summer months
our island teems with tourists of many nationali-
ties, some of whom do not display the attitude of
respect to which your sex is entitled.'

Birdie stared, then remembered just in time
that any show of amusement would be deeply
offensive to the man whose protective, dominat-
ing, possessive attitude towards women had the
effect of making her feel deeply aware of her fem-
ininity and caused wistful regret for the passing
of the poke bonnet and rustling crinoline. Her last
barrier of doubt fell when he rose to his feet and
with a slight bow requested in the manner of a
courteous grandee:

'Will you allow me the honour of escorting you
back to my home, Señorita Wren? Dolores, my
housekeeper, is waiting to serve tea.'

'But I've no wish to put you to further trouble,
señor!' A flutter of foreboding acted as a reminder
that the calmer the sea the more plentiful the
nets.

'It is no trouble,' he insisted briefly, helping
her to rise with a grip upon her elbow as silken-
tight as the cords once used by abducting Moors
to bind the wrists and ankles of reluctant captives.
A tremor ran through her body as he guided her
through the network of tables, then headed towards the narrow street where his home was
situated. But she submitted to his will with dignity, too proud to allow him to guess that her
pulses were racing, her heart hammering with the
anxiety of a small, trapped bird.

'I'm . . . I'm looking forward to seeing Lucita
again,' she spoke with determined brightness as

she was guided along whitewashed streets with an ambience of medieval calm that seemed to match perfectly the dark, Moorish profile of the man brooding silently alongside her.

'*Como* . . .?' He seemed to dredge his mind from a depth of thought. 'Lucita, did you say? I'm sorry, I'm afraid she won't be present. As she finds the heat of town so trying I have ordered her to rest in her room until we return tomorrow to the Casa de Solitario, our home across the bay. During the summer season when social life declines, everyone disperses to their various summer residences, which is why most of the houses you see around you are empty and silent, having perhaps one ancient retainer left in charge while the owners are away.'

'Oh, but I thought——' Birdie jerked to a halt when realisation dawned, reluctant to be entertained in a bachelor establishment, even one situated in the midst of a tightly knit labyrinth of aristocratic homes.

With embarrassing accuracy, he read her mind. 'Don't worry,' his tone was dry as he edged her through a wrought iron gateway and into the intimate little garden, 'tonight these secluded plants will exhale their passionate perfume into the air; night-flowering stock will open their petals to the moon; on the orange trees, buds will break to sweeten the warm night air with their heady scent, but unfortunately,' he mocked, 'you will not be here to share my enjoyment.'

Silently she wrestled with humiliation as he led the way into the library where a low table had been covered with a fine lace tablecloth set with a beautifully embossed silver tea service. When they were seated Dolores poured liquid amber tea into china teacups, then served dainty sandwiches on to matching Sèvres plates enamelled with the coat of arms of the de Retz family.

Dolores's expression was impassive as she waited on them, but a malicious gleam, quickly hidden, caused Birdie to suspect that the display of richness was a deliberate ploy on the house-keeper's part to make her feel uncomfortable, a reminder that nondescript strangers had no place among such aristocratic splendour. A silver tray deeply engraved with the motto: *Viget Inter Nubile Phoebus* added extra emphasis to the way of life to which the Conde had been born. *Phoebus shines between the clouds!* At that moment, in the depths of a sombre library, the sun-god, Phoebus, seemed to have been eclipsed by a servant's dark scowl and by the brooding shadow of a man so wrapped in thought he seemed almost to have forgotten her presence.

When the slender handle of her cup slid through damp fingers, causing it to make noisy contact with an equally fragile saucer, Dolores uttered a sharp cry of condemnation and darted forward as if to scold. The Conde's head jerked up and at the sight of Birdie's horrified expression he ordered coldly:

'That will be all, Dolores, you may leave us now.'

Shaken by the housekeeper's secret glare of malevolence, Birdie carefully deposited the price-less china on the table, then leant back with a sigh of relief, clenching trembling fingers in her lap.

'Dolores has served my family for so many

years she is inclined to take liberties,' he frowned. 'You must not allow her to intimidate you.'

'Considering I'm not likely to remain here for longer than an hour it hardly matters what your housekeeper thinks of me,' she returned lightly, wishing she had not allowed herself to be coerced into returning to his sumptuous establishment. For a second he seemed about to contradict, then he changed his mind and sank once more into a depth of reflective silence.

Birdie occupied her time during the uncomfortably long interval speculating upon the reason why the Conde's fire should suddenly have been reduced to a smoulder, then once that abortive exercise began to pall, she turned her attention upon a magnificent porcelain group set upon a nearby table, depicting a lithe, vigorous horseman pulling on the reins of a rearing stallion, the battle of strength between man and beast revitalised by a ray of sunlight glinting upon rippling muscles and taut sinews, adding an animated gleam to staring eyes.

She shuddered and turned away from the barbaric tableau, only to be confronted by the haughty stares of Retz ancestors whose painted faces were ranged around the walls—men with hooked, Moorish profiles, women of delicate beauty—all seeming to wear identical expressions of disdain.

She was just about to suggest that it was time for her to leave, when she was startled by his comment:

'You are a restful person, *señorita*, your physical gifts of lightness, grace and serenity more than compensate for your unfortunate tendency to speak bluntly.' He was lolling at ease, watching her closely through lowered lids, so could not have missed the sweep of hot colour in her cheeks nor the shy, almost hunted look that flickered into her eyes. 'What set of circumstances has combined to produce such a puzzling enigma?' he continued slowly, almost as if speaking his thoughts aloud. 'Your exceptional talent brought you almost to the brink of fame; you have withstood the spotlight of adulation without flinching, yet once off stage you creep into the shadows of anonymity, taking little part in conversation, seemingly content to remain quiet and overlooked. Your independent spirit allows you to wander through streets full of strangers, yet, as if determined to confound, you felt reluctant to accept an invitation to take tea once you became aware that there were to be no other guests present. What makes you such a capsule of contradictions, *señorita*? I know that as an artist you are called upon to play many different roles, but why do you insist upon extending that ability into your private life—is it that you feel naked when stripped of pretence? Is your own personality so colourless you feel forced to hide it, as a clown hides despair beneath a mask of paint?' He leant forward to probe her small, frozen features. 'Which, out of a conglomeration of graceful ballerina, disreputable, half-drowned trespasser and scatterbrained jaywalker, is the character one must cultivate in order to discover the real you?'

Soft lashes dusted hot cheeks but did not dare

to rise. 'You recognised me as the girl you almost ran down with your car?' she husked.

'Not I,' he confessed grimly. 'My nerves were too shaken by the near disaster to permit my mind to register any details of your appearance. No, it was the sharp-eyed minx Lucita, who was sitting in the rear seat of the car, who took note of your appearance, especially your slight limp, and who connected you with the incident immediately we were properly introduced.'

'You called me an idiot!' she accused, eyes hazel-bright with indignation.

'And various other names, under my breath,' he admitted without a trace of apology. 'I would not wish such a traumatic experience on any man. Truthfully, it can be said that you made a dramatic impact upon my senses from the first moment of meeting!'

'I'm sorry,' her blush deepened, 'I suppose the blame was entirely mine. Usually, I walk facing oncoming traffic, but because I was daydreaming I forgot that your traffic laws differ from those of my country and stepped into the road oblivious to the fact that a car was approaching directly behind me.'

'Fortunately, I react quickly to danger,' he sounded in no mood for forgiveness, 'but be careful in future that you do not test the ability of one who does not.'

She was able to smile because, although he sounded severe, he was obviously worried on her behalf. 'As my first—and probably my last—visit abroad is almost at an end, there will be little opportunity for the same situation to arise. However, I'll keep your warning in mind,' she promised, solemn as a child who has just been chastised.

For a second the corners of his mouth curled upward as if he was tempted to be indulgent, to smile in the manner Lucita would be quick to interpret as a sign of forgiveness, but though a hint of humour lingered around his mouth his mind seemed otherwise occupied.

'You are leaving soon, you say?' he frowned. 'But why? Only a couple of days have passed since your arrival.'

'Lady Daphne wants her yacht to be put through its paces,' she explained, 'and as we must return to London by the end of the month there's not much time left.'

'What is so significant about the end of the month?' he prompted.

'Rehearsals are due to begin,' her eyes lit up with an animated sparkle. 'Tony is anxious to start work on his new creation, a wonderfully witty production of *Coppélia*. My solo comes in Act Three—' she began, then broke off abruptly, her expression stiff with the shock of recall.

He did not even pretend to sympathise, indeed it was almost as if he wanted to stamp the painful reality upon her mind, to snap the last fragile thread that bound her to the world of ballet so that never again would she be able to pretend that some day, through some miracle, her ankle would be once more strong and flexible enough to allow her to dance.

'To have an ideal is the most important thing

in life, but that ideal does not necessarily have to be a career,' he stressed hardly. 'Some jobs can be achieved without driving passion or selfless dedication and yet be equally rewarding.'

'Such as . . .?' Her hazel eyes were sceptical.

'Such as helping a child to come to terms with a disability,' he stated calmly. 'I am ready to admit that I may have done you an injustice, Señorita Wren. Upon closer acquaintance, you appear to possess a *simpatia* for my ward that might be beneficial to the child. I have therefore decided to offer you the post of companion to Lucita—she will be left exclusively in your charge, no one but myself will be in a position to override your decisions. You will have ample time off, of course, and will be treated in every respect as one of the family.'

'No, thank you . . .!' She jumped to her feet incensed. 'I think you must have forgotten, *señor*, that I already have a job—as a *dancer*!'

She had not noticed how incredibly cruel his mouth could be until his lips tightened.

'On the contrary, *señorita*, you are the one who is refusing to face reality, you must learn to accept that it is no longer your destiny in life to dance the role of Odette in *Swan Lake*; the sleeping, beautiful Princess Aurora, or Romeo's youthful Juliet! I know what you are about to say,' he held up a hand to silence her shaken protest, 'but it would be the act of a coward to go back to the ballet world to be treated as an object of pity, to be dealt crumbs instead of cake!'

Birdie closed her eyes to combat the pain of hearing said aloud what she knew in her heart to be true and to shut out the sight of her taunting Spanish inquisitor. 'Tony said,' she gasped piteously, clutching the one remaining straw, 'that I could be——'

'His Coppélia . . .?' he interrupted hatefully. 'A girl with enamelled eyes, a lifelike doll with clockwork apparatus where her heart should be, who will move her arms and legs, even dance when she is wound up, who will talk and smile to order so that from a distance no one will guess that she is not a human being but a feelingless wooden puppet!'

'Stop . . .!' she cried out with pain, unconsciously pushing her arms outward with palms uplifted in a gesture of mime she had used many times on stage to convey horrified defence against a wall of invisible oppression. 'You're heartless,' she almost sobbed, casting a tortured glance around the luxurious room, 'all your life you've had everything you could possibly wish for, you've never had to live with the indignity of knowing that you were born unwanted, left on the steps of a Home, your only inheritance the contents of a cardboard box! You grew up in these surroundings,' she charged shakenly, 'so you can have no conception of life as it is lived in an institution where everything has to be shared, where a moment of solitude is a treasured luxury, where one's only personal possession is a toothbrush. I didn't merely work to achieve my ambitions, señor, I flogged my body to the brink of exhaustion, practising at the barre until my limbs felt tortured, studied until my mind felt crammed and my eyes felt gritty with lack of sleep—so why are you attempting to rob me of everything I've earned? Why are you determined to destroy my dreams, my hopes, even my dignity . . .!'

He rose to his feet, his autocratic features devoid of compassion. 'Dignity is a luxury you cannot afford, *señorita*,' he chided coldly. 'Instead of dwelling upon what has passed, never to be regained, you should be feeling grateful for my offer of alternative employment, for giving you an opportunity to retire with dignity from a scene in which you have no further part to play. Now is the time to face the fact that you have no wares left to sell in the market place of ballet. Once again you have been reduced to poverty,' stressed the inhuman Conde who would not be crossed, who expected to have his every whim fulfilled, 'everyone needs to eat—you will soon discover that it is impossible to exist on a diet of pride!'

CHAPTER FIVE

BLEAKLY, Birdie stared at the gradually lengthening wake stretching between Mahon and the boat that was speeding her across to the opposite shore where the Conde's villa stood in splendid, white-cubed isolation. The space where the *Terre-à-terre* had been berthed was now empty. Earlier that morning Lady Daphne's yacht had set sail with only herself and Tony on board.

During a farewell party the night before Birdie had been called upon to enact the most brilliant performance of her career, to play the part of a girl bemused by her good fortune at having been chosen by the Conde de la Conquista de Retz as a companion for his young ward. In reality, although she had smiled and chatted her way through the nightmare evening, accepting the good wishes and congratulations of the assembled guests, her movements had been purely mechanical, her senses numbed. But now the numbness was beginning to fade and she found herself alone, grappling with the agony of reliving the shock she had experienced after leaving the Conde's house on the day she had joined him for tea.

Quietly, unobserved, she had slipped aboard the yacht intending to make her way down to her cabin to lick her wounds in solitude. But then she had hesitated and changed her mind when she heard the sound of voices engaged in conversation coming from the direction of the main salon.

Recognising Tony's even drawl, she had veered towards the salon, eager to have her shattered confidence restored, to gain the reassurance that only he could give, but when she had almost reached the threshold Lady Daphne's clear voice had dropped a bombshell of worried questions into the quiet air.

'Can't you see how unfair, how positively cruel, it is to encourage the idea that there's room in the ballet world for a girl who's permanently crippled? Hasn't Birdie suffered enough without having the added heartbreak of being encouraged to return to London where, once pity wanes as it surely will, she'll become the butt of snide remarks, accusations of favouritism, and attitudes of intolerant contempt? The members of the corps de ballet can be made up to look like angels, but some of them are capable of acting like veritable devils towards anyone they think might be blocking their advancement. To appear in the spotlight even for a second is regarded as a great accolade, as you're very well aware, Tony, so how do you intend to protect Birdie from envy and spite whenever, as promised, she's favoured with minor mime roles?'

'I shall have neither the time nor the patience to become involved in such trivia, dammit!' Tony had exploded, 'nor am I prepared to begin worrying about a situation which I doubt will ever arise! Birdie may be quiet and self-effacing, but she's always commanded the highest regard from the rest of the company.'

'Because her talent demanded it,' Lady Daphne had reminded him quietly.

'And will continue to do so!' he had spat with a savageness that had betrayed his underlying anxiety.

It was then that she had crept out of earshot and stumbled down to her cabin to brood, to wrestle with an inner voice screaming that she must pretend not to have overheard, then finally to bravely come to terms with the unpalatable conviction that the Conde had been correct in his assumption that she had nothing of value to trade in the ballet market place. In only one respect had he been wrong—instead of the gratitude he had demanded, she felt a dislike akin to hatred for the man whose sword-edged tongue had slashed a chasm of uncertainty around her stumbling feet.

The Conde's manservant cut the engine of the boat and allowed it to glide to rest against a wooden jetty that seemed to be pointing an accusing finger into the pure aquamarine sea. A flight of stone steps led upwards from a crescent of silver sand protected from trespassers by yuccas and prickly cactus set against walls built from stone quarried out of the terraced hillside on which the villa was built. When they reached the top of the steps the man guided her along a path that wove through an orchard of almond trees, then petered out into a garden ablaze with colourful flowering shrubs set around a sward of finely-manicured lawn.

Sunshine beat down upon their heads as they trudged up an incline paved with warm patchwork stone, then when they reached the top he hesitated, swept his arm through the air, then waited with an anticipatory smile for her reaction.

In spite of her low spirits, her resentment at feeling trapped, she gasped appreciation when her eyes fell upon the house he had indicated. At close quarters, stark white walls outlined against a background of vivid blue sky were so hurtful to the eyes she turned with relief towards a pink-tiled swimming pool and a shady covered terrace floored with black slate flagstones. Moorish simplicity dominated the scene, tables and chairs of honey-gold cane were dotted around the terrace; potted palms with huge fringed leaves formed a restful contrast to the hot splash of geraniums against white walls. Window grilles, and decorative wrought iron lamps suspended from sloping beams, emphasised the Arabic ambience, as did a crudely coloured blanket hung upon a solitary expanse of wall, and low stools set around carved wooden tables where guests would gather to drink Turkish coffee or Moroccan tea after lunch or dinner.

A tall figure, his tanned features outstanding against the stark whiteness of a shirt left casually unbuttoned to the waist, strolled across the terrace at their approach.

'*Gracias*, Juan.' He dismissed his manservant with a nod before turning his cool blue gaze in her direction.

'So, Señorita Wren,' his smile was totally lacking in warmth, 'you have finally decided to make your nesting place in my home.'

'*Decided*, with its inference of free choice, is

hardly appropriate, *señor*,' she trembled, feeling lost and nervous as an abandoned fledgling.

'Were you abducted ...? Coerced ...?' he challenged thinly.

'No,' she sighed the admission, 'but very cleverly cornered, wouldn't you say?'

A squeal of delight forestalled his angry retort, and with relief she turned to greet Lucita who had erupted on to the terrace and was limping quickly towards her.

'Señorita Birdie!' she called in a high, excited treble. 'Is it true what Tio told me? Have you really come to stay with me for ever?'

'Not quite as long as that,' she smiled. Compassion for the crippled child welled up inside her as she dropped gracefully to her knees and held out her arms just in time to catch her small frame quivering all over with ecstatic joy.

'Oh ...!' Suddenly Lucita's face dropped, her small mouth forming a quivering moue of protest. 'But Tio said so, he *promised*,' she gulped.

When the threat of tears seemed imminent Birdie hastened to console. 'I'll stay for as long as you need me,' she promised rashly, then froze with foreboding when a glance of sardonic blue warned of quick retribution if ever she should be tempted to renege against her unwary statement. She wanted to bite back her words, to retreat from the trap of her own making, but he was quick to slam the door on his captive. With smooth, narrow-eyed insistence he set a seal upon her subservience.

'You can rest contented now, Lucita, little flightless one, for the *señorita* has given her solemn word, and if the English possess but one virtue it must be the virtue of integrity.' Obviously amused by Birdie's fiery confusion, he continued to mock: 'It is said that the English race is prepared to suffer unbelievable hardship in the cause of principle—it will be interesting to discover whether Señorita Wren's character provides us with proof of the maxim that every cask becomes infused with the qualities of the wine it contains.'

It was a relief to escape with Lucita, who was eager to lead the way up to a bedroom adjoining her own that had been prepared for her new companion. To one who had grown used to sleeping in dormitories, then latterly in a hostel room shared with three other girls, the spacious bedroom that would be flooded with sunshine immediately shutters were removed from its two windows; with its whitewashed walls, fitted wardrobes, shelves holding a selection of English novels, an abstract painting, a scattering of carved wooden animals, and a floor tiled in the same restful green as the traditional Spanish bedcover fitted neatly over a low divan bed, was almost enough to compensate for being cut off from the life she loved, wrenched from the niche in which she had been so happily entrenched.

'I helped to arrange the flowers,' Lucita prattled joyfully as she urged her inside to admire an urn spilling a profusion of blossoms; two geranium plants set in vivid ceramic pots, and a trailing ivy displayed on a wide shelf running the full length of one wall with the smallest window set in its centre, a chair of convenient height, a blotter, and a selection of pens and notepaper indicated that some thoughtful person had designated the shelf as a writing desk.

'How lovely ...!' Much to Lucita's delight Birdie seemed lost for further words.

'Tio and I spent ages discussing which colours would suit you best,' the mentally-mature child preened importantly. 'My bedcover and lampshades are red and I wanted you to have the same, but Tio said: No, a timid English wren might take flight and fly from a background that is too ex ... exotic,' she stumbled, then beamed, proud of having managed the awkward word. 'You are not feeling frightened now, are you, Señorita Birdie? I want you to teach me to be as graceful as a swan, I could not bear it if you should fly away.'

The child's obsessive awareness of her deformity was worrying. Birdie sank down upon the divan and waited until Lucita was perched alongside her. 'Your limp is very slight,' she assured her gently, 'even less noticeable than my own. As you grow older the muscles in your ankle will gain strength and quite probably the limp will disappear completely, so why don't you try ignoring it?' she suggested lightly. 'If you forget about it, then everyone else will.'

'Dolores does not think so.' She was shocked to see Lucita's bottom lip beginning to quiver. 'I heard her telling Juan that Tio will find it difficult to persuade any man to take a wife who is crippled. I don't want to grow up like Dolores,' she gulped, 'she has no husband, no children, so she finds it difficult to smile.'

Birdie, too, found it hard to smile, and even

harder to suppress the anger she felt for a household full of adults all so selfishly absorbed in their own affairs they could not spare the time to listen to and disperse the fears of an over-imaginative child. Dolores's remark was unforgivable, but the bulk of her anger was directed towards the Conde, whose negligence she blamed for permitting the child to be left too often within earshot of gossiping servants. Her main consideration at that moment, however, had to be Lucita, whose expression was betraying a sadness completely alien to a five-year-old.

'Let's explore the rest of the house,' she suggested brightly, rising to her feet. 'I'm sure you must have lots more to show me.'

'I *have*, I have . . .!' Lucita's volatile spirits rose. The pressure of excited fingers dug into Birdie's hand. 'You must see the room that Tio has had specially fitted out to help us with our exercises.'

Birdie was almost tempted to forgive the Conde his many faults when, after guiding her along the passageway outside of their rooms, Lucita ran ahead to fling open a door.

'Isn't it *splendid* . . .!' Rapidly she twirled her fingers through curls bunched either side of her head—an enchanting mannerism she adopted whenever she was highly excited. Barely able to contain her eagerness, she waited for Birdie's reaction to a room that was completely empty, its wooden floorboards bare, filled with ample light and space and with mirrored walls stretching the entire length of two practice barres.

Birdie's surprised expression and shining eyes

seemed to supply all the answers Lucita needed. 'Isn't Tio kind, Señorita Birdie?' she clapped, sparrow-hopping on the spot. 'I do hope tomorrow comes quickly, I can hardly wait to begin!'

'The *señorita* is not to be rushed, Lucita!'

Birdie swung round to face the approaching Conde, who eyed her with amusement, seemingly aware of the opposing factions of resentment and gratitude battling for supremacy inside her.

'Are you pleased with the surprise we planned for you, *señorita*?' he drawled. His mocking glint tipped the balance of her emotions in favour of resentment.

'The facilities appear to be adequate,' she said frostily, 'but I can't give a definite verdict until I've tried them out. If you wish,' she dropped her lashes, deliberately adopting the role of a newly-taken slave before a master she despises, 'I'll change into a leotard and practise a few exercises.'

'That will not be necessary.' Her heart kicked with triumph when he snapped his displeasure, then plummeted when he punished her gentle sarcasm by ordering Lucita, 'Dolores is waiting to serve your lunch. When you have finished it please take your rest without argument, *comprende*? Meanwhile,' he flicked Birdie a distant look, 'you will accompany me downstairs, *señorita*, we have many matters to discuss.'

Fearful of trying his patience too far, she obeyed without demure, following sedately in his footsteps as he led the way towards the terrace where a table had been laid and a servant was waiting to serve lunch. Throughout each course they conversed with distant politeness, but once she had disposed of a fluffy omelette stuffed with broad beans, and a strange, delicious dessert consisting of a long, narrow strip of puff pastry rolled in quince jelly and dessicated coconut, then topped with pieces of crystallised greengage, apricot and a whole preserved orange, he seemed to consider that the time was ripe to return to the attack. He waited until the servant who had served them with coffee had disappeared from view before commencing his startling attack.

'Now, *señorita*, I should like to be told the reason behind your sudden change of attitude towards my offer of employment. When you left my house in Mahon you were in no frame of mind to even discuss the matter, yet the following morning you wrote me a letter of acceptance. Why . . .?'

'Because I'd had time to think things over,' she replied levelly, determined not to be intimidated, 'to realise the truth of your claim that my dancing career was finished, that I had no family to turn to, no permanent home and no experience in any other type of work.'

'I see . . .' He nodded thoughtfully, yet still appeared unconvinced. 'And yet those same circumstances existed when you turned my offer down?'

Birdie hesitated, loath to disclose the conversation she had overheard between Lady Daphne and Tony, and too sensitive to perpetuate the lies she had told them about her eagerness to prolong her visit to Menorca, to enjoy the facilities of the Conde's luxurious home, to break away completely from a world in which she could no longer achieve success.

She took so long to reply that he prompted with rising suspicion. 'Well, *señorita*, I am waiting . . .?'

'I . . . I didn't want Tony to begin regarding me as an encumbrance,' she husked, her cheeks fired by a blush of humiliation. 'He's such a wonderful man, always so kind and considerate—especially since my accident—but I couldn't bear pity, not from him . . .' She stumbled into awkward silence.

'You mean your ambitions lay in other directions?' He sounded suddenly dangerous. 'Even though you must be aware of the deep attachment between Tony and Lady Daphne, you are gambling upon the chance that your absence might jolt him into realising that his feelings for you are stronger than mere affection?'

She stared, too appalled for words.

'You looked shocked, *señorita*,' he stated dryly, 'but then acting is part of your training, is it not? Unfortunately, you have not yet mastered the art of controlling a mercurial blush that acts like a barometer, defining your degree of emotion.'

The impulse to speak out in her own defence was killed by the force of her anger. The fact that he was now her employer did not entitle him to pry into her personal affairs, nor to demand insight into her private thoughts. Though he had jumped to a wrong conclusion she would not contradict him because she could not care less about his poor opinion.

'I had formed the impression, Señor, that the

object of our discussion was to outline my duties,' she dared to remind him, then tensed, sensing from his stillness that a terrible anger was about to erupt. But as she waited, terrified, an expressionless mask closed over his features, his blazing eyes became hooded.

'You are right,' he agreed tightly, 'it is time we moved on to more important business. What do you know about the after-effects of polio . . .?'

'Very little,' she gasped, 'except that often a limb is left paralysed.'

He nodded curtly. 'Mercifully, Lucita's infection was slight and once the inflammation died down her ankle, the only limb affected, began to show signs of functioning which proved that the nerve cells had not been destroyed. All that can be done now is to try to strengthen the weakened muscles. She has had courses of therapy, of course, but in polio more than in any other disease only thirty per cent of the cure depends upon the doctor, the rest depends upon the patient herself. Which is exactly why you are here, Señorita Wren. You are the last of a long string of helpers with whom Lucita has stubbornly refused to co-operate.' He pushed back his chair and with an air of preoccupation began striding the length of the terrace. She sat rooted, wondering if an attempt to escape would attact his attention in the way the flutter of wings attracts the sharp eyes of a prowling tomcat. She had almost decided to chance it when his prowling footsteps halted in front of her and she was forced to stare into his brooding eyes.

'There is a second reason for your presence

here,' he frowned. 'Lucita lacks the security of a family atmosphere—she needs to share the confidences of a sister, to learn to tolerate a brother's teasing, and above all she needs a permanent feminine presence to supply love and reassurance immediately it is needed. In the past, because of the child's possessive attitude, it has been difficult for me to introduce another woman into my household but now that she has transferred a great deal of her attention to you my task should be made somewhat easier. Can I rely upon your co-operation, *señorita*?'

'My co-operation in what . . .?' she stammered, completely at a loss.

'Surely I have made my meaning clear!' He bent towards her until his aggravated mouth was mere inches from her bewildered face. 'I am appealing to you for help,' he enunciated slowly as a teacher to a backward pupil, 'asking you to ensure that Lucita is kept fully occupied so that I am left free to concentrate upon the task of finding a suitable wife!'

CHAPTER SIX

THE *task* of finding a suitable wife! With which criteria would the Conde judge a woman a suitable candidate for marriage?

Throughout the previous evening while she had been left to dine alone, Birdie had pondered upon the cold-blooded attitude of the man whom she had earlier glimpsed making his way down to the jetty where a servant had been waiting to ferry him across the bay to Mahon. In spite of his white dinner jacket, knife-creased slacks and a dress shirt with cravat ruffling down to an elegant cummerbund, she had been reminded of a Spanish conquistador, one of the wild, ruthless men whose captives had been given the choice of becoming slaves or having their throats cut; who had drunk rum, fought duels, and plundered cities of their treasures. Which unsuspecting victim, she had wondered, was about to have her emotions besieged? How many ambitious fathers were about to extend hospitality towards a guest wearing a cloak of courtesy and charm, good manners and witty conversation, while carrying out a cool, calculating assessment of their daughters?

Yet in spite of her insight into his motives, in spite of her instinctive recoil against the idea of a planned, emotionless marriage, as the boat had sped away leaving a trail of frothing water in its wake, she had been annoyed by the unbidden thought that even when thinly spread the Conde's charm could be effective—*concentrated*, it would be deadly!

'Señorita Birdie, how do I look . . .?'

Jolted from her deep study, she spun round to examine Lucita's small frame poised to display a pale blue leotard. She nodded, suppressing her amusement at the vanity registering in every line of Lucita's body as she stood on tiptoe in unshod feet, a minute pair of ballet shoes dangling by their tapes from a limply outstretched hand.

'Very workmanlike,' she approved, then suggested tactfully, 'but just a little chilly so early in the morning, don't you find?'

Frowning, Lucita dropped her pose and advanced into the practice room, her expression openly critical of Birdie's outfit.

'Why are you wearing that clumsy woollen vest and thick leggings over your leotard?' she accused, her mouth drooping with petulance.

'It is normal practice for dancers to wear crossover bodices and knitted legwarmers at the beginning of a class,' Birdie enlightened gently, 'they help to keep unexercised muscles warm and are gradually discarded as the work-out begins generating natural warmth. Shall we try to find you some woollens?' she extended a coaxing hand in Lucita's direction. 'I'm certain there'll be something suitable in your drawers.'

'No,' Lucita pursed a mutinous bottom lip, 'I'm happy just the way I am—I don't feel the least bit cold.'

Birdie sighed, mentally preparing herself for

conflict. Though the atmosphere outside was warm, the sun had not yet progressed towards the back of the house where the room was situated and as a consequence, in just a few short minutes, Lucita's bare arms and legs were displaying evidence of goosepimpling. To have demanded obedience from the pampered infant would have been to court an undignified battle of wills, so instead she began sauntering towards the door in an attitude of negligent unconcern. 'In that case, I'm afraid I won't be able to help you,' she told the surprised child. 'A dancer's working day is organised to the exact minute, therefore the very first lesson that has to be mastered is the acceptance of discipline. Such a shame,' she directed a sympathetic smile, 'that one so keen to dance should fail at the very first hurdle.'

She had crossed the threshold and walked half the length of the passageway before her stubborn pupil decided to capitulate.

'Don't go, *please, señorita!*' Her cry rang out tearfully plaintive. 'If you wait just a second I'll fetch a vest and some stockings from my room!'

When the lessons eventually began it became evident, to Birdie's relief, that Lucita had absorbed the principles of discipline at her very first attempt, that the vain child who had pictured herself an instant ballerina had abandoned high-flown fantasy in favour of dedicated plodding, settling down with a gratifying show of concentration to practise the five basic positions of the feet that had been worked out to ensure that a dancer's balance remains perfect whatever the position of the body, positions with which almost all the steps in classical ballet begin and end.

Lucita was standing perfectly positioned, with the heel of her front foot 'locking' into the back foot's instep, when Birdie was startled by the sight of the Conde's image appearing on the mirrored wall. She kept her back turned when he stepped inside the room, but could not avoid the chilling blue scrutiny reflecting through glass.

'Tio, look at me!' Lucita rocked and almost overbalanced in her eagerness to attract his attention. 'This is one of the five positions that have been taught to dancers for over three hundred years!'

'Then they must be of the utmost importance,' he asserted gravely, his questioning eyes upon her teacher.

Sensing that some sort of reply was expected of her, Birdie turned reluctantly to face him. 'We must wait until Lucita is expert in these movements before we can begin proper training. You will notice, *señor*, how her feet are turning out from the hip at an angle? Not only will such exercises help her to achieve freedom of movement and an elegant appearance, they will also do much to strengthen her ankle. However, Lucita,' she turned with relief to address the child, 'you've practised enough for one day. As a beginner, you're bound to find the exercises tiring, so you must try to curb your impatience and be satisfied to make progress slowly.'

When Lucita's body slumped, the Conde forestalled her threatened protest.

'I'm pleased to hear you say so, Señorita Wren, because although I felt reluctant to interrupt your first lesson I became concerned that my ward might overtax her strength. Run along to your room, little workhorse,' his teasing charm seemed to work effectively even upon infants, 'and tell Dolores that before lunch you are to take a warm shower.'

He seemed taken aback when she obeyed—even responded with alacrity to Birdie's instruction to retrieve vest and legwarmers from the floor where she had dropped them, and with elevated brows he watched as she limped out of the room.

'What magic have you worked upon the child who, in the manner of wild cactus, has always refused to be trained?' he questioned dryly.

'No magic, *señor*. Lucita is simply responding to the appeal of the unusual. For the first time in her life she has been made to work to rule, and she enjoyed the experience because basically all children feel a need for discipline.'

She guessed from his frown that this concept was alien to his impulse to over-indulge his ward. 'I have always found Lucita more responsive to persuasion than to severity.'

'And it is my experience that a young branch will take on all the bends one cares to impose upon it,' she countered serenely, reflecting with gratitude upon her own rigid training, the alphabet of classroom steps that she had been made to practise until perfect because they formed the dictionary from which she was later to construct her choreographic sentences.

When his eyes pinpointed she moved away, unnerved by the frosty glance of a man unused to feminine argument, one brought up in the

Spanish tradition that whatever a man says is right—because he is a man. To punish her daring he employed a weapon against which she had no defence, a leisurely, studied appraisal of limbs laid bare to inspection by a leotard designed to give dancers complete freedom of movement, to enable teachers to examine every movement of the body and so spot mistakes at a glance. Birdie was used to such scrutiny, but never before had a critical eye forced upon her a need to fight an inner trembling, never had she felt stripped by a look of cool cynicism.

'So worldly-wise, yet so physically immature!' he mocked, skimming the surge of small breasts against flimsy material, an incurving waist, and shapely legs with the knowledgeable eye of a slave trader. 'In my country feminine slimness is regarded as a sign either of extreme youth or dire poverty.'

A blush rose under creamy skin, lashes swept down to screen telltale signs of panic beneath an agitated quiver, but the head on the slender, vulnerable neck remained unbowed, her reined-in voice remained steady.

'And in my country, señor, a man could make the same remark without fear of sounding hypocritical, for we English have a deep contempt of double standards. It appears to me that a curious feature of the Spanish man's conventions for women is that he applies them only to his own womenfolk—wives are treated like minors, consequently they permanently adopt the role of dependent children and in turn your children are reduced to the status of playthings. Yet you are quick to cultivate the acquaintance of girls who are not content to be mere animated dolls, to enjoy their intelligent conversation, even to entertain them alone in your bachelor apartments, when to suggest such a thing to a girl of your own race would be considered unthinkable! You may tell yourself that your traditional attitude of masculine possessiveness is prompted by chivalry, *señor*, but I am tempted to suspect that intelligence and artistic distinction is deliberately repressed in your womenfolk in order to perpetuate the myth of masculine superiority.'

It was doubtful whether the scion of the House of Retz had ever before suffered such a scathing condemnation of himself or his countrymen. In his eyes, woman had been created by God from Adam's rib in order to supply man with a companion, a comfort, a pleasant diversion—never with a critical equal!

Birdie held fast to her composure even when a thin blade of displeasure sliced above her head.

'You seem intent upon declaring war, Señorita Wren. In the past, many battles have taken place between our respective countrymen, but this time, if you insist upon resurrecting long-dead feuds, I must warn you there will be no surrender— Menorquin honour will be upheld whatever the extent of bloodshed!'

With her spirit in tatters she retreated to the security of her room, only to discover, as she stepped across the threshold, that she was once more within range of a barrage of Spanish fury. The door connecting her own room with Lucita's was open and the child's haughty treble was clearly audible.

'I do not have to rest after lunch today, Dolores, Señorita Birdie said so!'

'The *señorita* had no right!' The reply was spat with a fury that caused Birdie to quake, nevertheless she advanced into Lucita's room, knowing that to act the part of mediator was included in her duties. If she had stopped to think, her approach to Dolores might have been more diplomatic, but nerves still jangling from her confrontation with the Conde prompted the hasty interruption.

'Lucita is quite right in what she says, Dolores, I did promise——'

The housekeeper whirled in her direction, a black-clad vision of quivering indignation. '*La niña* has been my responsibility since she was an infant. I nursed her all through her illness and have seen to her wellbeing ever since without interference from anyone until you arrived! You are a bad influence!' she cried, her eyes small black buttons of sparkling jet. 'First you English came to Menorca to murder with cannon and musket, and now you come in your thousands, overrunning our island for six months of every year, corrupting our young men by parading almost naked and outraging their elders by displaying a disgraceful lack of decency!'

Birdie withstood the pointed reference to her revealing costume with a show of dignity she knew would have to be maintained if Dolores was to be prevented from claiming supremacy. 'I'm sorry you don't approve of me, Dolores,' her quiet apology left the housekeeper completely disconcerted, 'but I feel that any complaints you have to make would be better addressed to the Conde. Meanwhile, as only he has the authority to overrule my decisions, I'm taking Lucita into the garden where, as promised, I shall read to her for a while.'

Throwing a look of pure triumph towards Dolores, Lucita scrambled off the bed and ran to Birdie's side. But as neither the time nor the place was right, she stifled an impulse to lecture the child on showing respect towards her elders and as a balm to the housekeeper's pride instructed Lucita:

'You will apologise to Dolores for your show of ill temper, if you please, Lucita, and promise her that never again will you be guilty of disrespect.'

'But, Señorita Birdie, it was *she*——'

'*Discipline*, remember, Lucita . . .?'

The warning rang a bell. 'Very well.' With sulky ill grace Lucita turned to the simmering housekeeper. 'I beg your forgiveness for my ill manners, Dolores.'

'*Nada, nada buena chica!*' the housekeeper cried, casting a look of venom at Birdie as she brushed past her and ran out of the room, leaving her feeling drained by what she suspected had been a mere rehearsal of battles yet to come.

But by the time they had changed and made their way to the terrace to stretch out on a comfortable lounger with a parasol to protect their heads and a view of the pink-tiled swimming pool to lend an illusion of coolness, the problem of Dolores's hostility had been pushed to the back of Birdie's mind.

'From which book would you like me to read?' she invited when Lucita had snuggled close to her side.

'From the one containing stories about the ballet,' she promptly decided, then startled Birdie with the irrelevant statement, 'I have a brooch of painted enamel that once belonged to my *madre*.'

'How nice,' Birdie replied, momentarily at a loss. 'You must show it to me some time.'

'Enamel is hard, and so thick I cannot see through it. Does that mean that the girl in the ballet—the one with the enamelled eyes—was blind?'

'Do you mean Coppélia?' Birdie felt as surprised as she sounded. 'What can you possibly know——' She stopped abruptly when a notion struck her. She and the Conde had been alone when he had so cruelly likened her to the puppet heroine, nevertheless, only last evening upon checking Lucita's room and finding it empty, she had searched the house and discovered her tiptoeing along a passageway clad only in her nightdress, pausing outside of every door like a listening, inquisitive wraith.

'Lucita, have you been eavesdropping?'

The unrepentant child nodded. 'Before you came to keep me company I had nothing else to do,' she admitted cheerfully. 'Often, when the night is warm and I cannot sleep, I take a walk——'

'*And listen at keyholes!*' Birdie concluded wrathfully. 'Promise me you will never do such a thing again!'

'Oh, very well,' Lucita shrugged, 'I find grown-ups' conversation very hard to follow in any case, especially when they speak of a girl with enamelled eyes who has a clock where her heart should be and can only move when she is wound up. Please, *señorita*, will you explain to me the story of *Coppélia*?'

There seemed little point in prevaricating. Lucita's interest had been fired by snatches of conversation, but it seemed feasible to assume that once her curiosity had been assuaged she, unlike her insensitive guardian, would cease to connect the doll of the ballet's title with her unfortunate self. She sighed, wondering how members of the Retz family managed to become such adepts at getting their own way.

'Very well. Briefly, the story is as follows. Once there lived an old man whose name was Doctor Coppélius who studied ancient books on magic and hoped that some day he might become a famous magician. He was also an expert toymaker whose wonderful clockwork dolls could move their arms and legs and walk and dance about whenever they were wound up. He liked to pretend that they were real humans and that he was a magician who had endowed them with life, especially the doll he named Coppélia which, from a small distance away, could actually be mistaken for a real human girl.'

'Did she have real hair, Señorita Birdie, like my favourite doll, Juanita?'

'Yes, and rosy cheeks and deep blue eyes shiny as enamel,' Jennifer confirmed. 'When he set her on a chair on the balcony of his house people thought they were looking at a very lovely young girl who was always fashionably dressed. Sometimes the doctor would wind her up so that she danced, but mostly he left her sitting on the balcony with a book on her lap.'

'Did no one ever try to *talk* to her?' Lucita gasped, her eyes wide as saucers.

'Yes, a young man who had fallen in love with the beautiful puppet, but of course he never received a reply. His sweetheart, Swanhilda, was very upset about his switch of affection and being a sensible girl she even doubted that Coppélia was real—which was just as well, seeing the young man still had her to turn to when finally the truth about the inhuman puppet girl was finally revealed.'

Lucita's face dropped, showing her obvious dissatisfaction with the end of the story. 'But why wasn't the puppet girl brought to life?' she protested. 'In my book of fairy stories the heroine is always awakened from her trance by a kiss from a fairy prince.'

'Perhaps she was an English puppet, *niña*,' an amused voice interrupted, 'with a sturdy heart of oak and a disposition guaranteed icy enough to discourage even the most ardent suitor.'

Jennifer did not need to look up to discover the identity of the jeering presence whose shadow had invaded their pleasant surroundings. Hiding her intense resentment behind a barrier of downcast lashes, she returned his fire with a salvo of contempt aimed directly at his insufferable pride.

'There is a well-known English saying, *señor*: "Listeners never hear good of themselves". Obviously, as eavesdropping appears to be a national pastime, you will not be deterred by such a warning, but for the sake of Lucita who appears to slavishly follow your example, may I pass on to you another piece of advice that I had drummed into me during my supposedly deprived childhood, namely, that whoever interrupts the conversation of others makes notorious his own lack of breeding!'

CHAPTER SEVEN

A STATE of armed neutrality had been declared between the members of the household of the Casa de Solitario. A month had passed since Birdie's arrival, a time during which some ground had been gained and some lost; tempers had been curbed and occasional pleasantries exchanged, but always in the background, insidious as the beat of muted drums, lay the threat of conflict, the danger that one unguarded word, one unconsciously-taken liberty, would bring a speedy end to the armistice.

Lucita, however, was progressing well with her lessons, so well that the Conde had become disturbed by the keenness of her dedication and sought out Birdie in order to confide his worries. She found it impossible to emulate Lucita's habit of taking an afternoon siesta, therefore she was filling in time sewing new tapes on the child's ballet shoes when the Conde appeared beside her on the terrace.

'There is no need for you to do that,' he frowned. 'I did not employ you to do the work of servants.'

'I don't mind, *señor*. A dancer always sews on her own tapes, she alone knows where they will feel most comfortable. Also, if she does the job herself no one but she can be blamed if the tapes should work loose during a performance.'

She schooled her fingers not to tremble when

he sat down beside her, her composure strained to the limit by the close proximity of a man who for the past weeks had seemed to go out of his way to avoid her company. Of course, the task of finding a suitable wife must have been keeping him fully occupied. Each evening he was transported by boat across the bay to Mahon and back again to the villa in the early hours of the morning. Business, she assumed, kept him occupied during most of the day, and yet there had been a puzzling lack of visitors to the Casa de Solitario. By this time, she had imagined that a troupe of would-be *condesas* would already have been paraded for Lucita's approval, but as yet not one likely candidate had appeared on the scene. Perhaps, she had finally concluded, he had decided to be more cagey, to conduct his courtship in secrecy before presenting his *novia* as a *fait accompli*.

'I must congratulate you, *señorita*, on your expert handling of my precocious ward. Your assumption that she would respond well to discipline has been proved correct. The child looks happier than I have ever seen her, also her manners have improved immensely.'

The needle slipped, pricking deep into the soft flesh of her finger, yet it was her heart that reacted to the jab of his unexpected praise. 'Why . . . why, thank you, *señor*, it is very generous of you to say so,' she mumbled, keeping her eyes averted from the lounging frame emitting a threat of piracy even though clad in a casual black shirt and well worn denims—an outfit that gave fair indication of his intention to remain at home for the rest of the day.

'However,' he hesitated, choosing his words with care, 'although your tuition has improved Lucita's deportment—I have noted that she is no longer inclined to drag her foot, as she used to—I think it would be a great mistake if she were to be buoyed with false hopes of growing up to be a ballet dancer.'

Carefully, Birdie laid her work aside. 'You do me an injustice, *señor*, if you imagine that I have not taken great care to ensure that Lucita is completely aware of her limitations. After all,' her eyes reflecting the soft brown look of a hurt animal reproached him, 'who should know better than I the pain of hopes destroyed, the utter aimlessness of a life deprived of the stability that comes from the knowledge that one has a useful role to play in life, that, though never indispensable, one is at least needed.'

'You miss the ballet world very much, don't you?' Keenly, he held her gaze, forcing her eyes not to waver, demanding entry into her very soul. 'Can nothing ever take its place—a husband, a home, children, perhaps?'

For a long shaken moment while his glance remained locked with hers she felt a rising tide of hope, a lifting of depression, then memories came flooding back of the bustling rabbit warren of a world that forms the backstage of a theatre—painters transcribing an artist's small design into a huge, bold backdrop; carpenters hammering in thousands of nails; frantic costume staff hard at work turning designers' sketches into garments eventually to be worn by the dancers. Then again, the sounds of a ballet about to be born, an orchestra tuning up; excited conversation humming through the theatre before lights faded, the conductor entered the orchestra pit and, seconds later, the curtain rose . . .

'Birdie, *tell me*, would they be consolation enough?'

As if from afar she heard the Conde's voice, felt the grip of his fingers on her arm as he willed her to answer. The shock of his touch, the surprise of hearing him speak her name without the usual formal prefix caused an emotional upheaval far greater than the trauma she had experienced the night she had waited in the wings for the cue that had signalled her debut as a solo dancer. She reacted with panic to the stirring of numbed emotions, to the tingling of nerves that had lain dormant since the doctors had imparted their crippling diagnosis. *She did not want to be brought back to life, to suffer more pain!* All she wanted was to be allowed to continue playing the role of Coppélia, the wooden puppet who could not be hurt because she had no feelings . . .

'*No!*' she cried out in fear of being made to come alive again. 'No, that's not what I want!'

'I'm sorry, I did not mean to cause you distress.' He loosened his grip upon her arm. 'Your seemingly calm acceptance of the bitter-sweet of life led me to hope that sufficient time had elapsed to ease a little of the regret imposed by the collapse of your career and by the absence of the most important person in your life. Obviously, I was wrong . . .' He jerked to his feet and in a couple of pantherish strides reached the edge of the pool. 'I feel in need of a swim,' he decided, 'would you care to join me?'

'I can't,' she gasped, nervous of his caged-in virility, 'I don't know how.'

'You have never been taught to swim?' he swung round to question incredulously. 'I have always considered it a first priority for people who live on an island.'

'I never had time to spare for swimming lessons,' she defended uneasily, sensing that he was angry yet at a loss to understand why.

'You have time to spare now,' he told her pointedly, 'if you change into a swimsuit we can begin to rectify the omission.'

The very idea of such shared intimacy was horrifying. 'No, thank you,' she declined swiftly, 'I don't think I want to.'

'But I want you to, *señorita*,' he insisted silkily. 'I refuse to leave my ward in your sole care until I can be certain that she is in no danger of being left to drown.'

He left her with no option but to obey what was tantamount to an order. Seething with resentment of his high-handed command, Birdie went to her room to search for her one and only swimsuit, a modest white creation hastily purchased upon receipt of Lady Daphne's invitation to join her cruise. Because she was nervous of deep water she had worn it only once, on the day she had escaped to the beach in an attempt to avoid the tea party aboard the yacht, but as her time had been spent dabbling in the shallows before she had scampered out of the storm, the suit had remained unmarked and looked satisfyingly pristine.

She was confused by the degree of shyness that

overcame her whenever she felt the Conde's eyes upon her naked limbs. Modesty could not be tolerated on stage where dancers of both sexes were called upon to perform in costumes often explicitly revealing, yet his most cursory glance imposed upon her a paralysing embarrassment rendered all the more unbearable by the certainty that he was aware of and amused by it.

She had to force herself not to flee when she returned to the pool and caught sight of a brown forearm cleaving through the water; a spume of water raised by his kicking foot, a flash of narrow, black-clad hips and lean thigh when he reached the end of the pool and did a somersault underwater. Teeth glistened white in a smile when he caught sight of her, correctly reading apprehension in every line of her tense figure.

'Of what are you afraid, *señorita*?' he grinned, hauling himself out of the water. 'Here there are no sharks lurking in the depths, nor even tiddlers flirting in the shallows.'

Birdie could have replied with truth that the shark she feared most was human, a man who was a reputed master of the *piropo*, the flattering phrase, the flirtatious quip, which he could use with devastating effect if ever the mood should take him. Instinctively, she backed away from eyes that were suddenly alive with devilry, from lips that looked ready to tease, to wreak havoc under the pretence of murmuring encouragement.

Her worst fears were confirmed when his towering, seal-dark body drew close enough to allow him to slide a loose arm around her waist.

His touch had the effect of cold steel against her warm body. Suddenly as his fingers made contact with her skin every nerve and sinew brought to the peak of suppleness by years of dancing practice stiffened, making her retreat look clumsy, jerky as the response of a puppet to the tug of a string.

She writhed with embarrassment when he laughed aloud at her discomfiture and fought to curb the rise of colour that he had learnt to tap at will in order to judge whether her emotional state was inclined towards fair, unsettled or stormy.

'Before I can begin to teach you anything, you must learn to relax,' he reproved, thoroughly enjoying his dominance. 'As water is an element strange to humans, one must learn to adapt one's movements to its properties. With beginners, fear is the commonest cause of inability to relax, the mind reacts upon the body and increases muscular tension, breathing becomes erratic, the pulse rate responds as it would to danger or,' he glinted, 'to a state of high excitement. Take a deep steadying breath,' he commanded, nodding approval of her instinctive response. 'Now expel it slowly and at the same time allow your muscles to relax. Feel better . . .?' he prompted.

'A little . . .' she gulped the lie.

'Good. Now you must trust me, leave yourself entirely in my hands. I promise that you will come to no harm.'

Birdie decided that that was one instruction she would never be able to follow, yet after negotiating the steps leading down into the shallow end of the pool she followed him without fear, her hand grasping his, until the water began to submerge her shoulders.

'Jump up and down until you become used to the feel of water on your face, keep your eyes open, and breathe out into the water while your head is submerged.'

She ran the tip of her tongue around dry lips. 'You'll stay with me?' Her anxious brown eyes begged for reassurance as she stood poised on tiptoe, her head tilted to avoid the lap of water against her chin.

His smile was unexpectedly tender, and she was glad of any excuse to plunge underwater, to avoid the scrutiny of eyes so often stormy and turbulent, but now sparkling as sun on a deep blue sea without a breeze to ripple its surface, no outburst of hail to chase warmth from its depths.

The moment the water closed over her head, however, she was assailed by a different sort of panic, a purely physical fear of being out of her depth, left floundering in the clutches of a heavy alien mass that was dragging at her limbs, blocking her nostrils, squeezing every drop of breath out of her lungs. Frenziedly she jerked out of his grasp, desperate to have both hands free to fight her way back to a surface that suddenly appeared to have receded far above her head, and continued to recede farther and farther out of her reach. Just when her lungs seemed on the point of bursting she was plucked out of the depths and held with her head above water until her paroxysm of coughing and spluttering had died down. Fear of being released, of plunging once more into dangerous depths, drove her to abandon all sense of reason. Immediately the Conde's dark head appeared in focus she flung her arms around his neck and clung tight as a limpet to his rock-hard chest.

His gasp of surprise, the bracing of his muscles, ought to have served as a recall to sanity, but she felt too stripped of confidence, too shocked to think straight when she stormed at the satanic face mere inches away:

'You promised not to let go of me! I ought to have known better than to trust a cold-blooded devil who sets about choosing a wife with the same dispassionate interest he would show when shopping for a suit. Sadistic brute . . .!' she spluttered, outraged, 'a girl would have to be out of her mind to marry you!'

Her aim was to exact revenge, to wipe the infuriating grin from his face, but even she was surprised at the speed with which laughter lines vanished from his face, by the instant immobility of his body, by the disappearance of forked amusement, suddenly eclipsed by a cloud of feeling that dulled his brilliant eyes to grey. The fact that she had overstepped the boundary marking the dividing line between employer and employee had barely time to register before his arms began tightening around her slim waist, gradually increasing their pressure until she was trapped in a bone-crushing embrace that shot a thrill of terror through a body fluttering pale as a butterfly pinned to a dark, unyielding frame.

Mesmerised, she stared into his eyes as his face drew nearer and nearer until their lips were almost touching. She could feel the coolness of his breath fanning her cheek, sensed his savage impulse to kiss any further insults from lips quivering slightly open as she began breathing faster and more deeply. She closed her eyes to shut out the sight of a determined mouth lowering to punish, but the crush of his kiss put an end to her darkness. Brilliant light flared, flooding every secret part of her young, immature body, delving into the depths of her soul, melting the ice around her heart, sapping every ounce of energy from limbs that felt boneless, filling her mind with the discovery of a depth of passion she was encountering for the very first time.

She had to resist a compulsion to protest when he lifted his head, his expression reflecting the reluctance of a man drawing back from mortal temptation, and managed to fight her way back to reality, to smother a longing to dwell upon an instant of shared enchantment she knew she would never be able to forget as long as she lived.

The Conde, too, seemed to be having difficulty in concentrating his mind, but after fraught seconds when they seemed to be in danger of drowning in the seduction of rose-tinted water lapping their bodies with the warmth of tepid wine; of an atmosphere hung heavy with the scent of blossoms, still and silent except for the fluttering of dove-grey wings and the humming of bees sipping from flower to flower, he reached out a hand to administer a paternal pat upon her cheek and instructed in the gentle, affectionate tone he generally reserved for Lucita:

'Time to get dressed, *niña*. Your first lesson is

over, you must not risk catching a chill.'

There seemed little likelihood of that when her
body felt stoked with heat from an inner furnace
that had been kindled into life by a kiss and was
now ablaze with flames threatening to consume
her entirely. But she was given no chance to argue.
Bodily he lifted her out of the water and deposited
her at the side of the pool while he fetched a towel.
She shivered when he draped it over her head
and began to rub her hair dry, a shiver of apprehension born of a suspicion that one could
never be certain what the Conde would do next,
that his quicksilver nature was so unpredictable
he could revert from saint to sinner in seconds.

Conforming to her theory, he stopped rubbing
and held the edge of the towel in a bunched fist
beneath her chin, so that her troubled face
appeared framed by a coif.

'Must you look like a possessed nun awaiting
the expulsion of the devil?' he chided roughly,
then immediately relented when he saw her flinch.
'It was never my intention to upset you, *niña*,' he
continued more gently, 'but you do seem to
possess an extraordinary ability to get under my
skin. We Menorquins are a passionate race, but
unfortunately the tree of passion has been known
to yield both bitter and sweet fruit in the one har-
vest. Can you forgive me . . .?'

Native pride reared when she interpreted
warning in his words, an implication that the
small interlude was relatively unimportant, a lapse
of manners he would prefer her to forget as
quickly as possible.

'Certainly,' she shrugged, managing to appear

unconcerned, 'after all, a kiss can mean anything or nothing—an oath; the sealing of a promise; a confession of love, or, if the kisser should happen to be a rogue, a reminder to a girl to count her teeth. My teeth are all intact, *señor*.' She flashed a brilliant smile to prove what little harm had been done.

'Together with a complete set of claws,' he murmured dryly, releasing his grip upon the towel so that she was able to escape beneath its folds.

Birdie concentrated with unnecessary vigour upon towelling her hair dry, hoping he would leave before the activity became so prolonged its objective would be revealed as a ploy to hide her mortified expression, to act as a barrier between herself and the man who could fire dangerous emotion into the heart of even a lifeless doll. Cautiously she eased up when a long silence seemed to indicate that she had been left alone, but was consequently all the more startled when she emerged from under the towel and discovered him sitting opposite, quietly watching.

'Have you taken a day off since your arrival here?' he frowned, blue eyes stern.

'I haven't yet felt the need,' she defended in a voice jerky as her heartbeats. 'My duties are pleasant and far from tiring.'

'That may be so,' he rose to his feet to tower over her, 'nevertheless, as I have no wish to earn the reputation of being a slavedriver, I insist that you take adequate time off to enjoy yourself. For the rest of today you must feel free to do exactly as you wish. I will attend to Lucita—then this evening,' he hesitated slightly, then issued a startling invitation, 'if you will permit me, I will take you to Mahon where we can dine together before visiting an unusual nightclub which I'm certain you will enjoy. Would you like that?'

He made no attempt to touch her, no effort to coerce or cajole, but merely waited, narrow-eyed, watching expressions of amazement, doubt, and then finally shy pleasure chasing over her expressive face. She knew it would be foolish to accept, dangerous as a child playing with fire, yet some inner yearning prompted rash words of acceptance from her lips even while her mind was urging caution.

'You are very kind, *señor*,' she stammered in her confusion. 'Thank you, I should like that very much.'

CHAPTER EIGHT

SHAKING with reaction, Birdie flew to her room, as breathless as if she had climbed her first mountain, swum a wide stretch of sea, and flung herself on to the bed to contemplate the possible consequences of the only reckless act she had perpetrated in the whole of her young life.

What had possessed her to step within the clutches of a man she had dubbed a dangerous autocrat from the first moment of meeting, a man who had made no attempt to disguise the resentment he felt towards every one of her countrymen, or his personal, puzzling dislike of herself? He had offered her employment simply because he could not help himself from indulging the whims of the child whose mother had been the only woman he had ever loved. Her loss had turned him into a man of stone, a cold, unfeeling statue dedicated to the memory of a girl so dear to him he had not attempted to put anyone in her place—until now, and only because he had decided that Lucita needed a mother.

A dozen times during the rest of the day while she attended to her nails, washed her hair, or simply gazed out of the window indulging in the luxury of solitude, she took up pen and paper to write the Conde a cowardly note telling him she had changed her mind. Yet by the time the sun had dropped behind the horizon and lights shining from the windows of Mahon were reflecting on the surface of the darkened bay, the note was still unwritten.

'It's too late to back out now!' she admonished the frightened face reflected in her mirror, then stared long and hard at an image—insubstantial as a wraith clad in a mist of pale grey chiffon, skin magnolia-pale against hair parted severely, folded in wings either side of her head, then scooped to the nape of her neck where it lay folded into a soft chignon—thinking the apparition alien, one she could not possibly relate to, because the stranger's tremulous, pink-tinted lips were *smiling*!

In a panic of confusion she turned her back upon the mirror that seemed to reflect the prophecies of a crystal ball to pick up an evening bag that matched perfectly with shoes fashioned out of soft grey kid, then she drew in a long, steadying breath before leaving to keep her appointment with the impatient Conde.

As she descended a staircase leading down to a hall whose darkness seemed intensified by light filtering from a solitary Moorish lantern, she thought it was deserted until she heard the sound of footsteps and saw a tall dark figure emerging out of the shadows. When the Conde reached the foot of the stairs she hesitated before negotiating the last two steps, poised timid as a dove, its feathers ruffled by the draught from a predator's wings.

'Don't take fright, *señorita*,' he teased lightly, yet with a confusing lack of humour, 'though I must admit to a healthy appetite, I promise not to gobble you up.'

Appreciatively, he eyed the slow rise of colour that told him he had interpreted her indecision correctly, then continued observing her closely while, with an air of graceful dignity, she drew towards him.

'Your movements are a joy to watch.' The huskiness of his voice set her pulses fluttering. 'The control one senses is wonderful enough, but more wonderful still is the faultless artistry you bestow upon even the most mundane tasks. Sometimes,' he utilised the opportunity of helping her into her coat by bending close enough to murmur into her ear, 'I feel privileged as a ballet-lover being allowed to watch a performance enacted solely for his own pleasure. Did you know, *niña*, that often, when you are lost in thought, you adopt a beautiful repose that brings to mind a statue of faultless beauty, that when you drop down on your knees, absorbed in play with Lucita, I am reminded of the slow sinking of a cloak to earth, as in one of your dances, its ripples as moving to the spirit as a soft, seductive passage of music? Are you human, I wonder,' he quizzed whimsically, 'or are you a spectre of enchantment sent to bewitch us?'

The fact that she had understudied the role of Cleopatra, Serpent of the Nile, and mastered it to perfection, helped her to slip his seductive net with an aplomb that would not have disgraced the notorious queen.

'If only your words could be put to music, señor, you would make your name as a composer.' Gravely, she paid tribute to the man whose dedicated study of the *piropos* had made him an expert flatterer. 'But if any credit is due it must be given to my teachers who not only developed my talent but taught me that dancing helps to cultivate the soul and feeds the imagination, so enabling us to live completely.'

'Is that why you have now decided to opt out of life entirely?' he chided, swinging her round to face him. 'Others besides yourself have coped with frustrated ambitions without sinking into an apathetic limbo. There is no security on this earth,' he reminded her pointedly, 'so when the plate of opportunity is being passed around you would be wise to stretch out your hand when your turn comes and accept your portion gratefully.'

Birdie winced from his snap of words and from the pressure of fingers clenched upon her shoulders with the fierceness of a man desperate to hammer down some barrier that was impeding his progress. Then suddenly he released her and stepped away, once more the urbane, wholly-contained Conde with an appreciative eye for beauty.

'Forgive me, *chica*, for submitting you to a lecture, there will be other opportunities to discuss whether you should choose a life of turbulence or tranquillity. I should like you to remember this evening only with pleasure.'

A light breeze teased her hair as he led the way through the garden and down to the beach where the empty motor launch was bumping gently against the jetty. He helped her aboard, then left her installed inside the cabin while he went aloft to take charge of the controls. Great gusts of cloud were chasing the moon across the sky, alternately covering and uncovering it with their shadows, as he opened the throttle wide. Birdie peered through a porthole and felt a wrench when she saw the lights of the Casa de Solitario disappear behind a blind of darkness, leaving her feeling cut off from all that was safe and familiar, cast adrift on dangerous seas in the company of a man who she suspected had inherited all the characteristics of his namesake, Vulcan, god of fire; conquistador: a Spanish conqueror whose pleasure it had been to invade where he was not wanted, to exploit the defenceless with a ruthless lack of pity.

Their crossing to Mahon was smooth and so swift that barely ten minutes had passed by the time, as if determined to lay old ghosts of her past, Vulcan skimmed the motor launch to a standstill on the exact spot where the *Terre-à-terre* had been berthed. A taxi was waiting for them on the quayside, and as he helped her inside his eyes scoured her face made wistful by revived memories.

'You miss your friend Tony, *señorita*.' It was not so much a question, more a flat, terse statement of fact.

'Very much,' she confessed sadly, making no attempt to prevaricate. Tony had been part of her life for so long that his absence and all that it implied had left a dull aching void in her heart.

'Some wishes are best left ungratified.' In spite of his promise to make the evening a pleasant one he frowned darkly. 'You may feel certain that you know what you want, but I suspect you may have been influenced towards wanting what you are supposed to want. Your friend symbolises everything you have lost, the excitement of the ballet world; the heights you can never reach; the applause of an appreciative audience and the fame that follows such acclaim. If you imagine that all those things can be regained simply by marrying him then forget it,' he told her brutally. 'A man can appreciate cool, classical beauty on stage, he might even be prepared to worship at the feet of a dancer capable of projecting the rare qualities of purity and perfection that are sadly lacking in our imperfect world, but the place for statues is in churches—a man needs a warm, caring woman to share his bed!'

As the taxi wove its way through narrow, darkened streets he left her to reflect in shocked silence upon the truth contained in cruel barbs which, had she really been in love with Tony, would have shredded her hopes to ribbons. The Conde possessed a cruelty that was typical of his race, she pondered bleakly, keeping her head averted as the taxi sped quietly along cobbled alleyways that once had rung with the clattering hooves of Arab stallions carrying hawk-faced Moorish riders, each with a piece of feminine booty thrown across his saddle.

Had any of those girls, plucked from the security of loving homes, fallen in love with their ruthless captors? And if they had, had they perversely kept that love a secret, even to the point of encouraging the lie that their heart was in another man's keeping—*as she was!*

The notion that her emotions would in any way run parallel with those of a slave-girl was so distasteful she shuddered, but luckily the Conde's attention was directed towards the taxi driver who had drawn to a halt outside a hotel with a surprisingly modern frontage of black marble surrounding huge plate-glass doors.

'*Espera, por favor,*' he instructed the driver to wait. Then with his hand clasping Birdie's elbow he guided her inside a cool foyer, its stretch of black marble floor dotted with cream leather armchairs placed intimately around low tables of beaten brass.

'Would you care for a drink before dinner?' Taking her acceptance for granted, he led her towards a secluded corner and when they were seated instructed a hovering waiter, 'La Ina, por favor,' without consulting her wishes.

Ruffled by his autocratic assumption that he knew best which drink she would enjoy, she protested mildly:

'I haven't yet sampled the local Sangria; I'm told it tastes delicious.'

'An innocuous wine cup awash with lemon juice and sugar,' he dismissed contemptuously, 'a most unsuitable pre-dinner drink. On the other hand, La Ina, a pale, dry fino sherry produced in the vineyards of Southern Spain, is a wine so delicate and well-balanced it can be enjoyed at any time of the day and is especially ideal as an aperitif. One day, I will take you on a visit to the *soleras* where the best of our wines are produced.'

With lazy amusement he eyed the sudden blush that suffused her cheeks when he so casually intimated his intention that their relationship should extend into the distant future.

'*Soleras* . . .?' she stalled, willing her whirling thoughts to settle.

He nodded, amused eyes too perceptive for comfort. 'The *solera* system is the process of progressive ageing and blending that produces fine sherry. The *soleras* themselves comprise tiers of oak casks, each tier containing wine of a different age. Wine is drawn off for bottling from the oldest barrels in the bottom tier, which are then refilled from the next oldest barrels in the second tier. And so the progress is repeated, so that new wine takes on the older wines' character in taste, colour and bouquet, enabling outstanding quality to be maintained.'

Relief arrived in the guise of a waiter carrying a tray containing a bottle and two stemmed glasses. The Conde poured the wine himself, a thin, transparent stream of liquid that filled the fluted glasses with a pale golden glow. Tentatively, Birdie sipped and was surprised when the wine trickled cool as spring water down her throat, leaving a pleasant, delicate taste upon her tongue.

'Well, what is your opinion . . .?' With an assured smile he awaited her verdict.

'It's nice,' she confirmed, then, when his eyebrows rose, she qualified, 'I . . . I like its fresh, subtle smell.'

'Bouquet,' he corrected, his smile widening into a grin. 'Never, I beg of you, tell a winemaker that his wine smells!'

'Perhaps I'd better not drink any more.' Huffily, she set her glass down upon the table, made to feel extremely foolish. 'I seem to be conforming to the adage, *Wine can of their wits the wise beguile*.'

Quickly his smile faded. 'But the quotation also

concludes: *Can make the sage frolic and the serious smile,*' he told her gently. 'Which is why, *señorita,* it would please me very much if you would finish your drink.'

They were halfway through their meal, seated in one of the secluded alcoves lining the walls of a dining-room given a strictly traditional air by starched white tablecloths, glistening silver, sparkling glass and a bevy of soft-footed waiters ministering to the need of a solidly respectable clientele, when she was startled by his half jesting, half serious request. She had just responded to his query about whether or not the *fabada*—a spicy bean dish containing a varied assortment of poultry—and meat was to her liking with a polite and truthful, 'Yes, thank you, *señor,*' when an exasperated sigh forced her to look up with apprehension.

'Am I so terrifying that you find it impossible to use my name? Say it!' he ordered peremptorily. 'I promise the word Vulcan will leave no scar upon your lips.'

It was an impossible request, yet one that she knew she dared not refuse. All during the meal he had been very attentive, advising her on a choice of dishes, topping up her glass with a delicious red wine he had chosen especially because her taste was inclined towards sweetness, and carrying on light, interesting conversation so that eventually she had felt able to relax, even to laugh a little at his quips. But the effect of the wine was heady, which was why, combined with the Conde's intoxicating charm, she found it less difficult than she had imagined to stammer:

'Very well. The *fabada* is delicious, V . . . Vulcan.'

A diamond sparkled in his cuff when he lifted his glass in a mock salute to her courage. 'And may I now be afforded the same privilege as my ward by being permitted to call you *pajaro gris*, little grey bird?'

It was not fair, Birdie thought, staring into his brown lean face with brows winging blackly over eyes alight with teasing blue flame and a mouth holding a quirk of amusement that obliterated the thin line of cruelty that appeared whenever he was riled, that a devil seemed always possessed of far more charm than a saint!

With the sound of heartbeats pounding in her ears she managed to whisper: 'You may call me by whichever name you wish, but I would not have suspected you of being a romantic, Sen . . . Vulcan.'

'All Menorquins are romantic,' he assured her, his glance daring her to look away. 'The secret of our island's enchantment is that she is a woman and so to all males born within her boundaries she is a song we love to sing; a *novia* who responds to our yearning for love. A sweet secret nestles in her heart, the secret of loving, so whether you leave or stay, *mi amor*, your heart will remain forever in our island lost in the middle of the sea.'

Birdie was bemused with wine, charm, and pretty *piropo* by the time they left the hotel and slid once more into the taxi that was waiting to take them to a nightclub, as he had promised. When he laid an arm across the back of the seat, loosely encompassing her shoulders, she felt too relaxed to draw away, too drowsily contented to listen to a breeze that seemed to be sighing a warning, or to wonder why the interior of the cab seemed filled with the pounding of one huge, solitary heart.

When he kissed her for the second time that day she knew that she was in love with him—a kiss that brushed featherlight across her temple, as different from the first as honey to acid, as a gentle caress to a stinging slap, as a hymn to a bawdy sonnet. All day she had been struggling towards the realisation. Because there had been no parents to shower her with affection; because the attitudes of those chosen to look after children in care had, of necessity, to be strictly impartial in order to avoid any accusation of favouritism; because dedication to her work had taken precedence over teenage affairs, his first kiss had been the only one she had ever experienced—her introduction to a strange, new gamut of emotions that she ought to have recognised because through the medium of dancing and mime she had portrayed them all: the delight of Psyche being united with Cupid; the yearnings of the Lady of Shalott; the wanton abandonment of the Foolish Virgins. But now she knew that all that time she had been performing in the manner of a Sleeping Princess under the spell of the ballet. Only now, after years of waiting, had her prince arrived with a kiss of love to awaken her to ecstasy . . .

He had promised that she would find the nightclub he had chosen unusual, but she was unprepared for surroundings that seemed more of an extension of a dream, an enchanted grotto gouged half-way through a rugged cliff jutting far out over the sea. Concealed lighting highlighted the strata and picked out fossils compressed within ceiling and walls that flowed, dipped and curled, making her feel spirited beneath the waves of a petrified sea. Tables and stools that might have been fashioned out of driftwood were dotted around a floor strewn with seaweed, and around the perimeter of a stone dance floor, rubbed slate-smooth by dancing feet, flowed a shallow trickle of water which, besides adding enchanting authenticity to the surroundings, provided men with an ideal excuse to lift their partners into their arms and carry them in one giant stride on to the dance floor.

When Vulcan led her, starry-eyed with wonder, to a table placed in the centre of a jutting balcony, its front wide open to the sea and with only a flimsy wooden handrail and the suck and hiss of sea around rocks hundreds of feet below to add an intrusive note of warning, she imagined she had been spirited into the realm of Neptune and would not have been in the least surprised to see an elderly, bearded man of stately mien approaching, astride a dolphin.

A balmy breeze teased the chiffon collar of her dress, moon-silvered shadows lent a fey, haunting quality to her face as she gazed in wonder at a huge golden moon suspended from a black velvet sky casting a blanket of sparkling prisms over a heaving, slumberous sea.

'Shall we dance, *mi amor*?' He tendered the suggestion softly, as if aware of her mood of enchantment and feeling loath to break the spell. Mutely

she nodded, then with a sigh of pleasure rose to
her feet and drifted light as a wraith into arms
waiting to lift her inside a circle of bewitchment
where they danced together in enraptured silence
to music blending with the song of the sea, float-
ing and gliding as on the smooth crest of a wave,
their steps merging as one in a seductive rhythm
that sent shivers of rapture through her body and
set her spirit soaring as she revelled in a brief in-
cursion into Paradise. She longed to stay for ever
in his arms, dancing as she had never danced
before, without the need to concentrate upon
movement or direction, conscious only of the man
whose lips were brushing her temple, whose deep,
low voice was murmuring enticing Spanish
endearments in her ear, whose arms were a haven,
promising the home she had never had, the love
she had never known . . .

All spells must fade, yet some of the magic still
lingered when he escorted her back to the table
set secluded as an eyrie on a cliff top and discovered a smiling young flower seller waiting by
their table. Blossoms were spilling from a basket
hooked over her arm, velvet-petalled roses, a
crush of clove-scented carnations, sprays of vivid
golden-heart anemones and tight bunches of wild
violets all vying in colourful, perfumed splendour.

But without hesitation Vulcan chose a single
exquisite madonna lily with which to pay tribute
to her virginal young beauty. 'Simplicity adorned
is simplicity destroyed, child's heart,' he explained his choice with a depth of sincerity that
left her shaken. Then, taking her hand in his, he

waited until they were alone before adding what she considered was an entirely appropriate ending to the magical love scene. 'There is no better partnership than a good marriage, *querida*, two lives joined without a scar, two hearts beating in agreeable unison, don't you agree?'

'Yes, Vulcan,' she nodded, starry-eyed.

'Good!' He glinted his approval. 'In which case I take it you will raise no objection if our betrothal is kept brief—just time enough to arrange a quiet, informal wedding?'

CHAPTER NINE

SLOWLY, early morning sunshine awakened Birdie from a sleep so calm and sweet she had to struggle back to reality, to convince herself that the events of the previous evening had really happened and were not part of an extravagant dream. But as she turned her head sideways a tender smile crossed her face at the sight of one pale madonna lily, poised graceful as a ballerina on pointe set in a vase at her bedside.

So she hadn't been dreaming! A sigh almost of fear fluttered in her throat as she stretched out a hand to pluck the flower of enchantment from its resting place, to press her lips against its velvet petals and make a wish—a wish that soon she might be clasped once more in the arms of the impatient, masterful Conde who had decided to make her his wife, and be swept once more into Paradise.

Reality intruded in the shape of Lucita, an early riser, who had formed the habit of catapulting her small, warm body into Birdie's bed as soon as she awoke each morning.

'Señorita Birdie!' Bright, anxious eyes scoured her face. 'Why are you smiling?' Lucita sat back on her heels, cheeks pink as the ribbons threaded through the collar of her nightdress, and looked hesitant, conscious of some difference in the profile that looked sketched with a fine nib against the pristine pillow, yet unable to define it in

words. But when in one relaxed, graceful movement Birdie raised herself upright so that her
unpinned hair fell in a smoky brown mass around
her shoulders Lucita immediately decided, 'You
look exactly like the picture in my story book—
the one of the Sleeping Princess awakening from
her spell after being kissed by her prince. Have
you been kissed by a prince?' She bounced upon
the bed, clapping her hands with excitement, then
stiffened as if struck by some unpleasant reminder.

'What's wrong, Lucita?' Birdie slid an arm
around the child's shoulders, alarmed by her expression of dismay.

'The princess in my story book is carried off by
her prince to a land far away,' she gulped, bottom
lip trembling. 'Is that what will happen to you,
señorita, even though you promised to stay with
me always?'

'*Tonta!*' Birdie scoffed, gently deriding, then,
understanding the over-imaginative child's need
to be convinced, she continued to tease, 'I'm
human, remember, not a fictitious character in a
fairy tale. You may pinch me if you need proof—
but *gently!*' she cringed in mock-alarm from
Lucita's mischievous fingers, then collapsed with
her into a laughing heap.

Lucita, however, was as tenacious as her guardian in the pursuit of personal satisfaction. After
an interval of noisy play she returned to the subject that seemed to be always uppermost in her
mind, the fear of losing her teacher, her playmate,
the one person in her adult world whose background qualified her not only to recognise but to

indentify with her childish fears.

'When Tio marries,' she startled Birdie with a sudden return to solemnity, 'will you also come to wherever the new Condesa decides to send me?'

Birdie's breath caught sharply at this insight into a young mind instilled with poison dropped from the tongue of a woman jealous of her privileged position, a woman who had not hesitated to twist an infant's fears into a weapon guaranteed to rout any would-be usurper. Suppressing a tremor of anger, she attempted to undo the harm inflicted by Dolores. Given a choice, she would have nurtured her secret a little longer; the knowledge of Vulcan's love was so new, so precious, she wanted it to remain locked in her heart, to be taken out and examined at leisure until she had grown accustomed to the riot of emotion that weakened her body whenever she thought of him. But Lucita's need was greater than her own; she could not nurture her own joy at the expense of the child's unhappiness.

'The future Condesa has no intention of sending you away, *niña*. Indeed, although she and your guardian are very much in love their happiness would not be complete without you.'

Instant fear flashed into Lucita's eyes, a look Birdie had no trouble interpreting as the fear of insecurity, the terrible loneliness of the unwanted that had plagued her for most of her life.

'How can you possibly know, *señorita* Birdie?' she pleaded, white to the lips. 'Dolores says——'

'Dolores knows nothing of your guardian's business,' Birdie forestalled firmly. Opening her arms wide to the trembling child she spelled out slowly, 'Believe me, *chica*, I am telling you the truth.' A pink blush unfurled in her cheeks when shyly she confessed. 'Subject to your approval, of course, *I* am to become the new Condesa.'

The pandemonium that erupted gave proof of Lucita's joyous approval. With a scream that seemed destined to bounce for ever from walls and ceiling, she flung herself into Birdie's arms to babble, almost incoherent with excitement:

'Will the wedding take place soon? Am I to be a bridesmaid—can I wear a long frilly dress and help to carry your train? Will there be a big party, and if I promise to be very good will Tio allow me to stay up late? Will you have babies—lots and lots of real live babies for me to play with?'

At this, Birdie found breath to protest, 'Calm yourself, Lucita!' fighting to appear composed even though her pulses were racing, her mind jolted into realms which, as yet, had not even tentatively been explored. But Lucita's excitement was too great to be contained. With a whoop of delight she rolled out of reach to indulge in a frenzied orgy of bouncing at the foot of Birdie's bed.

'*Madre de Dios!* Have you taken leave of your senses, *niña*?'

Dolores's eruption into the room caused a sudden dramatic silence. 'You may think yourself safe because El Conde's room is out of earshot,' she snapped at Birdie, 'but when he is told of this disgraceful exhibition I have no doubt that he will dismiss you instantly.'

'No, he will not!' Lucita sprang back to life to

taunt her tormentor. 'Tio wishes to marry the *señorita* and I am going now to give him my permission!'

Dolores stood in aghast silence while a small tornado swept past her, then turned eyes mesmerised with shock upon the slender girl whose tilted chin was defying her to guess that her fists were clenched beneath the bedcovers.

'So,' she hissed, her back ramrod stiff with rage, 'you have done what you no doubt set out to do—achieve the distinction of becoming the Condesa de Retz even though you can never be accorded the respect that accompanies such a title!'

'What are you implying?' Birdie faltered, her courage cowed at the sight of thin lips stretched into a smile projecting more triumph than a grin, 'I love El Conde and he loves me.'

'*Que impertinencia!*' Dolores dismissed her claim. 'El Conde's heart is buried with the *novia* he adored, the mother of the child whose welfare is his main obsession. Ask yourself, *señorita*,' contemptuous eyes flickered over her shivering body, 'why he would contemplate marrying a nondescript English girl when he has a choice of girls from the best Menorquin families at his disposal? He does not need a wife in the physical sense, for over the years there have been many who have shown themselves willing to assuage his masculine appetite. All he seeks is a companion for the child, one who has attained the age of maturity yet retained the simplicity of an infant; one who is too self-effacing to demand attention and too lacking in feminine appeal to make any sort of impact upon his senses. You match up to

those requirements exactly,' she sneered. 'El
Conde will be well pleased with his choice once
you have learned never to step out of place, to
remember that he wants you not as a wife but
merely as a playmate for his ward!'

When the door banged behind her, Birdie
dropped back against her pillows, shaken by the
venom that had spurted from the tongue of the
woman who had sized up her victim well enough
to realise that she could mouth insults without
fear of reprisal. Quivering from the hurtful barbs,
she sought desperately to restore the torn fabric
of her dream, searching the dim recesses of her
mind in an effort to recall the exact words Vulcan
had used when he had tendered his proposal. But
though the impression of his hands was branded
upon her body, though his low, impassioned voice
echoed sweetly in her ears, though his hawkish
features and eyes blue as a Moroccan sky were
imprinted upon her heart for ever, she could not
recall one word of love from a mind reduced to a
bemused furore by intense looks and flattering
piropos.

Deciding that she had attached too much importance to the opinion of a jealous servant, she
attempted to dismiss Dolores from her mind as
she showered and then slipped into a sundress
pale as cream, with a belt to match her flat-heeled
tan leather sandals. As Lucita had not reappeared,
she wandered downstairs, then out on to the terrace where a table was set for breakfast. The
smell of freshly-roasted coffee beans and rolls
hot from the oven enticed her footsteps to
quicken, then jerk to a shy halt when she

spotted Vulcan, dressed casually in tee-shirt and
denims, seated at the table engrossed in his morning paper.

He rose to his feet immediately he caught sight
of her perched on one leg, employing the mannerism she had unconsciously adopted since her
accident of massaging her injured ankle with an
upraised foot.

'*Buenos dias, cara!*' For some reason he looked
amused. 'You look poised for flight, must I scatter
a few crumbs to entice you nearer?'

Birdie almost turned and ran, overwhelmed
with shyness, but he grabbed her by the waist, as
if guessing her intention. 'Did you sleep well, *mi
cara*?'

My darling! The endearment cancelled out all
Dolores's innuendoes and filled her with an exquisite sense of wellbeing. If he had intended her
status to be that of a superior sort of servant he
would not have addressed her so!

'Yes, thank you, Vulcan.' His name tasted sweet
on her lips. 'When I awoke I couldn't believe . . .
I thought I'd been dreaming,' she blushed pain-
fully, 'until I sniffed the air in my room and discovered it was heavy with the scent of a flower
which seemed to me to crystallise the very essence
of our perfect evening.'

She heard his quickly indrawn breath and dared
to look up with the quick loveliness of a glance
that could only be bestowed upon a lover, aware
that she was leaving herself vulnerable, but too
convinced of his love to care.

'Last night was no dream, *niña*, dreams are
limited, lacking in emotional sustenance; my pro-

posal was reality and so too was your acceptance. I take it,' he sounded almost too casual, too suddenly still, 'that you have not come to tell me that you have changed your mind?'

'I can't,' she admitted simply, 'Lucita has been told. Haven't you seen her . . .?'

'Unfortunately, yes,' he groaned, pulling her close so that his lips could trace the slender, graceful curve of her neck, turning her every bone to water, 'but I bribed her with a promise that she could be a bridesmaid at our wedding, provided she amused herself in the company of Juan's family for the rest of the day. Tomorrow, the world can intrude as much as it likes, but today I want to explore your mind, to delve your soul, and perhaps to make a little gentle love,' he husked, 'to entice you with kindness, a crumb at a time, until my timid English wren becomes tamed.' Sensing her confusion, he raised his head to examine fiery cheeks and agitated downcast lashes. 'Look at me, *mi cara*,' he demanded her complete attention, then when she met his eyes he bent his head to groan against her trembling mouth, 'Ah, *querida*, I want to share with you a delicious secret—the oldest, richest secret in the world, that love is sweet!'

Breakfast, to Birdie, tasted of coffee and kisses, fresh rolls and warm, loving glances so that when they left the table, hand in hand, she was too bemused to ask why when Vulcan led her away from the terrace and inside the casa.

Because nothing is more relaxing than the patio of a Spanish home, a courtyard open to the sky which, in the warm Menorquin climate, provides all that is needed for daily existence, she had rarely ventured into the downstairs rooms and was therefore surprised when he ushered her inside a study, a book-lined room dominated by a huge desk and a high-backed chair upholstered in dark red leather with a headrest of heavily-carved wood.

'Sit there,' he nodded towards the chair, 'there is something I want to show you.'

She did as he had instructed and immediately felt lost, swamped by the ambience of magnificence into which he had been born but which made her feel an intruder, as uncomfortable as a beggermaid wearing shoes that did not fit.

'One of my conquistador ancestors, together with two hundred others, made the perilous voyage to the South American continent in search of El Dorado, the legendary city,' he told her, placing a brass-bound box on the desk and inserting into the lock a heavy brass key that turned smoothly even though, to her uninitiated eye, the box appeared to be of great antiquity. 'Instead, they found the Inca civilisation in Peru, and it was from there that they returned with jewellery fashioned from pure gold, a metal worshipped by the Incas because they regarded it as an earthly manifestation of the sun. I should like you to choose a piece as a betrothal present. They are all much too heavy and ungainly to be worn in public,' he reassured her with a smile, 'but for my own personal pleasure I should enjoy seeing you wearing this piece, for instance . . .'

He lifted out of the box a broad gold anklet chased with a design of flowers and birds and knelt down beside her to withdraw the sandal from her uninjured foot. He must have noticed her recoil when he snapped the band of bondage around her ankle, yet he seemed pleased with the result, even tipped her foot higher, as if the golden shackle enclosing the slender, bird-boned limb excited his admiration.

'Take it off, please, Vulcan,' she begged, chilled by a superstitious shiver.

'Why, don't you like it?' His eyebrows met in a frown.

'It's beautiful . . .' she hesitated, 'but barbaric. Didn't primitive races hold a belief that all personal items should be buried with their dead owners?'

'Perhaps,' he shrugged, 'but they also believed that jewellery possessed magical powers. They wore amulets as protection against misfortune and the displeasure of the gods, as well as to display status and wealth.'

The coolness of his tone, his apparent indifference to her sensitivity shocked a resurgance of doubt and distrust of the man she knew she loved but whose mind she had never really plumbed.

'Do you really love me, Vulcan?' she whispered shakily. 'Am I to be a wife, or are you merely using marriage as a means of securing a permanent companion for Lucita?'

He straightened, and walked towards the window so that his expression was hidden and only his cold, emotionless tone registered on her mind.

'Marriage presents a way of solving both problems at one and the same time,' he shocked her by saying. 'For both business and social reasons I need a hostess who can put my guests at ease and carry out all the social duties that are beyond the capabilities of a housekeeper. Lucita, as I have already pointed out, needs the sort of security that can only be gained from being part of a family, which is why, although our marriage will be one of convenience in the literal sense, it must also be physically consummated if the family of Retz is to be provided with an heir.'

Numb with disbelief, Birdie stared with the eyes of a wounded animal at the implacable line of his shoulders, bewildered by the man who was a mixture of devil and saint, friend and foe, charmer and calculating schemer.

'It appears to me that in outlook you have not advanced far from the days when Spanish inquisitors resorted to torture as a means of breaking the will of anyone brave enough to oppose their views,' she choked. 'But you must realise that as a member of a civilised race who believes in the sanctity of marriage I find such sentiments appalling.'

He swung on his heel to face her. 'Then your knowledge of English history is obviously shaky,' he charged. 'Until your first divorce court was established some one hundred and fifty years ago an Englishman could dispose of his unwanted spouse quite legally, provided he was wealthy enough to afford the cost of the process. Even in the minds of poorer people it was firmly established that a wife was a chattel to be bought and sold in the same way as any other goods, and it was habitual for any man in search of freedom to take his wife to market—just as he would drive a pig—then after paying a toll which gave him the right to sell merchandise, to parade her around the market place extolling her virtues to any interested bidders. In spite of your accusation of patronage towards our womenfolk, *señorita*, we Spaniards have never been guilty of subjecting our wives to such indignity. Even the slave girls of our Moorish ancestors were cosseted in luxurious harems!'

'Slavery is a weed that flourishes in Spanish soil,' she countered bitterly. 'Your countrywomen have been conditioned to wearing the yoke of tyranny, but mine are too far advanced in intelligence and status to countenance such servitude, which is why I consider your proposal insulting and have no hesitation in turning it down!'

'You cannot!' His mocking conviction sent a spear of fear through her tense frame. 'You have informed Lucita of our wedding plans, remember? Also you promised to stay with her as long as she wants you to. I know that you will keep that promise,' he smiled thinly, 'because your tender conscience would not allow you to live in peace with the knowledge that you had broken the heart of a child!'

CHAPTER TEN

'No, I will *not* wear blue silk!' With all the petulance of a spoiled child determined to have her way, Lucita stamped her foot and glared at the dressmaker who was holding out a swathe of materials for her inspection.

Birdie sighed, wearied by the constant battle of wills being waged between herself and the two arrogant members of the Retz family. One painful surrender had already been forced upon her, but this skirmish was one she felt she must win if only for the sake of bolstering her shattered morale.

For some reason Lucita had decided that she wanted to attend the wedding dressed in the manner of a sugar-plum fairy and nothing, it seemed, was going to deter her from accepting anything other than a white net frou-frou.

'In order to achieve the desired effect, a frou-frou must be worn with satin pointe shoes, darling,' Birdie coaxed, 'and though these may look very elegant when worn by dancers on stage their blocked toecaps make them uncomfortable for normal walking. You wouldn't like to have to follow me down the aisle limping from the pain of a strained ankle, surely? Also, if fatigue should cause your limp to become exaggerated, a long skirted dress would help to hide it.'

Indecision wavered across Lucita's small, stubbornly-set features. 'Well . . .' she pondered, 'you could perhaps be right.' She cast a reluctant glance over the swathe of pastel-coloured silks. 'But not the blue—it's too cold a shade to be worn for a wedding, maybe pink would be better . . .'

Heaving a secret sigh of relief, Birdie turned away, leaving the patient dressmaker, who had been transported from a fashion house in Mahon, to cope with Lucita's tantrums. Her own decision had been made in a matter of minutes. A plain satin gown cut simple as a habit had seemed to suit perfectly her feeling of being cut off from the outside world, of preparing for a lifetime of servitude, duty, obligation, and the relinquishing of all hope of personal happiness. The tyrant had chosen his victim with care, binding her, tightly as any conquering Moor, with silken cords of conscience, concern and integrity.

Thankful for a respite from having to project the happiness of an eager bride, she moved across to a window and pressed her burning forehead against a pane of cool glass while for the umpteenth time she revived the painful conversation that had revealed Vulcan's true nature as well as the reason behind his deliberate assault upon her youthful emotions. She could not condemn his loyalty to Lady Daphne, a lifelong friend, but he had sounded vengeful, as if the Menorquins' centuries-old defeat at the hands of the English still rankled, when he had replaced the rejected anklet inside the brass-bound box and indicated coldly:

'It appears you have inherited the English trait of always managing to appear shocked whenever the tables are turned, allowing the victim to adopt the methods of his aggressor. Did you ever stop to consider the effect of your infatuation for Tony upon Lady Daphne?' he had asked her tersely. 'Undoubtedly, she must have recognised the threat presented by a much younger woman determined to practise her wiles upon a man already rendered susceptible to her advances by a guilt-ridden conscience, otherwise she would not have proffered the suggestion that you would make an ideal companion for my ward.'

'Oh, no . . .!'

'*Yes*,' he had insisted firmly. 'Naturally, pride would not allow her to admit such fear in so many words. Also she is of too generous a nature to act unkindly towards a fledgling who has toppled from its nest and is desperately searching for support for a broken wing.' Suddenly he had surprised her by allowing his attitude to soften slightly. 'Perhaps, in the circumstances, your panic was not so unforgivable. Marriage to Tony must have appealed as a solution to loneliness, insecurity, and lack of one person to whom you could truly feel you belonged. According to Lady Daphne, Tony is wedded to the ballet, and yet I have no doubt that a passionless half-loaf would have been looked upon with gratitude by a girl such as yourself who, given two loaves, would sell one to buy flowers.' He had loomed down until his aggravated face had entirely filled her vision before clamping: 'All things considered, isn't it just as well, for your own sake, as well as for Lady Daphne's, that I am in a position to offer you a more suitable alternative?'

An alternative form of torture! She closed her eyes in reaction to the pain of knowing what it is like to be a slave, to bear abuse and contempt, to feel trapped inside a cage of conscience that would not allow her to inflict upon a child the same sort of deprivation she had suffered herself, to be aware that although the door of her cage stood open she could not fly away because in spite of being made to quiver in the cold draught of his displeasure, in spite of bewilderment, of a timid fear of rough handling, she was too much in love with her jailor . . .!

Suddenly the atmosphere inside the room became oppressive, the swathes of material, the piles of patterns, the dressmaker's arch looks and meaningful comments to the prospective bride, and Lucita's ceaseless chatter about the wedding—a subject she had dissected so thoroughly it was now as tattered as Birdie's nerves—combined to form a suffocating pressure that caught her by the throat, making her gasp for air. Guessing that Lucita's preoccupation with her dress could be extending for another hour, she swung away from the window to voice a swift apology.

'Please excuse me, it's so warm in here, I must get a breath of fresh air. When you've finished, Lucita, you'll find me down by the swimming pool!'

Without stopping to listen to Lucita's half-hearted protest she sped out of the room, down the stairs, and on to a deserted terrace where sun-loungers were placed invitingly along the edge of a pool transformed by sunshine into a length of shimmering pink silk. She hesitated, then almost of their own accord her feet impelled her forward along patchwork paths that ran the length of the garden, then plunged downward through an almond orchard before petering towards a flight of stone steps leading down to a beach of silver sand.

Slipping out of her sandals, she ran barefoot down to the sea, scooping up the hem of her ankle-length cotton skirt to tuck it inside the waistband while she enjoyed a deliciously cool paddle.

The sea was so calm, the sky so cloudless, the breeze so light and sweetly caressing, she found it difficult to understand why Menorca should deserve its title of the Windy Island, or to imagine it as she had heard it described, being battered by the Tramontana, the boisterous north wind whose attacks were so menacing the islanders found it necessary to go all over their homes to close, bar and tie up anything that might yield to its fury. But the winter of black skies and dark gloomy sea, cold and swelling into towering mountains and deep abysses, seemed a thousand years away until the sound of a voice reaching from behind her caused the sun to grow cool and the sparkling to disappear from the glorious day.

'You remind me of a schoolgirl playing truant!' Vulcan's amused eyes sparkled over her bunched-up skirt and lingered for a second upon the curve of breasts outlined by a tightly-stretched cotton tee-shirt. 'Are you enjoying your paddle, *niña*?'

She swung towards him, resentful of being caught at play by a watcher standing with feet astride, his bare chest a symphony of coffee-coloured skin over rippling biceps; faded denim straining over muscular thighs and tapering shins, his savage masculinity made to appear even more

aggressive by a flat diaphragm cinched by a
leather belt decorated with rows of sadistic studs.

'Are you implying that I'm infantile?' she asked
stiffly, then was annoyed when she realised that
she had left herself open to a charge of petulance.

His sparkle of amusement faded, leaving his
face grave, almost sombre. 'On the contrary, I
believe that your normally happy nature has its
roots in an ability to retain a streak of childishness
to balance the weight of maturity. The childishness I was referring to was not the immaturity of
one who has resisted the pain of growing up, but
the conscious childishness of an adult whose un-
inhibited enjoyment of small pleasures is a joy to
watch.'

Birdie blushed, made to feel small, clumsy,
guilty as a chastised infant. Her awkwardness
must have been communicated to him by the
dejected droop of her head, by the way she was
paying fixed attention to toes curling in and out
of damp sand, because he chuckled, then jeered
softly:

'You worry too much about adverse opinion,
cara, too much of your life is devoted to pleasing
others, to subjugating your own needs! Why not
try being selfish for a change—and least some of
the time?'

'I have . . . I am being,' she admitted, shame-
faced. 'I've just fled from the house and left a
poor bewildered dressmaker to Lucita's not-too-
tender mercies.'

Vulcan threw back his head and laughed.
'Good! Then why not sell your soul completely to
the devil and come fishing with me?'

Seemingly deaf to her protests, he hustled her along the length of the jetty where, instead of the motor launch she was expecting, a *falucho*, one of the small boats with oars and a lateen sail used by local fishermen, was riding the swell. She was lifted inside and left to admire unobserved his suntanned body with muscles of steel, his assured, agile steps as he cast off and handled the sail, the way his dark, handsome face relaxed into a look of boyish enjoyment as his task absorbed the whole of his attention.

They had sailed out of the harbour and passed the buoys before Birdie actually became conscious of movement. The sea was delightfully calm and clear as they left behind sunburned rocks, winding lanes and villages with whitewashed houses inhabited by simple fishermen and their families whose height of ambition could be achieved by one exceptional catch that could be bragged about in the cafés at the end of the day.

Face downward, she leant over the side to plunge her arms into the warm water, endeavouring to catch in her hands one of the small fish teeming just beneath the surface. Exhilarated by a marvellous sense of freedom, she drew back inside the boat to unpin her hair, then lifted her face towards the sun so that long dark brown tresses were caught and teased by the stiffening breeze.

'Are you warm enough?' Vulcan called above the throb of a small outboard motor, his glance questing the surge of perked-up breasts and along the elegant, slender sweep of bared neck and shoulders.

'Perfectly,' she nodded, forcing back an embarrassed blush, attempting, and failing miserably, to meet the challenge of his audacious eyes.

'Good! I'll cut the engine once we reach my chosen fishing spot, then we will be able to talk without strain.'

She doubted the truth of this statement, yet strangely, after taking advantage of currents that helped him to navigate with meticulous precision towards his favourite fishing ground he had placed his lines, then dropped down beside her with a sigh of deep satisfaction, she found it easier than she had imagined to lean back against a pile of fishing nets and question curiously:

'I'm not in the least surprised to discover that you're a proficient sailor, but which expert taught you the art of fishing?'

'My grandfather,' he grinned, his teeth flashing white as the wings of a passing gull. 'He retired early, leaving his business affairs in the hands of my father so that he could be free to devote his time to his greatest pleasures—sailing and fishing. I was his constant companion, from him I learned how to handle sails, how to remove a hook from a struggling fish, how to read, hours in advance, from the humidity of the air, the state of the clouds, the flight of the gulls, any threatened changes in the weather.'

'It must have been wonderful to have had such a grandfather,' she sighed more wistfully than she realised.

'It was,' he nodded, reading the message of regret written across her lonely-orphan's face, 'but now that you have been convinced that marriage to me is your best option, I will endeavour to ensure that you don't miss out on the pleasures of being a grandmother.'

She stiffened, jolted from the dangerous lethargy engendered by euphoric surroundings, a feeling of comfort she had never known as a child, of being cosseted, rocked in a cradle of deep blue sea with golden sunbeams for a coverlet and heat haze hanging like protective gauze.

'I'm far from being convinced that there are any personal benefits to be gained from giving in to emotional blackmail,' she corrected coldly. 'I've agreed to marry you only because I feel certain that to go back on my promise, however mistakenly given, would inflict great distress upon Lucita.'

She was saved from his displeasure when his attention was caught by a tug of activity on one of the lines, then animosity became submerged by excitement when she responded to his instructions and attempted, a little squeamishly at first, to reel in the fish that had descended in a swarm upon the bait. Within ten minutes the bottom of the boat was filled with jumping, gasping fish, their rapidly flashing fins sparking brilliant, metallic colours as they caught the rays of the sun.

Birdie was flushed with exertion by the time Vulcan pronounced himself satisfied with the day's catch.

'Time for lunch,' he grinned. 'Are you hungry?'

Her breakfast had been frugal, yet she felt reluctant to admit to gnawing hunger. 'I'll survive,' she prevaricated lightly. 'Don't curtail your pleasure on my account.'

'I don't intend to,' he glinted, pausing in his task of shovelling fish into a wickerwork basket. 'Pleasure can be found even in a storm-beaten ship, if one is blessed with the right companion.'

Though she took care not to show it she glowed with happiness at the compliment, sensing, as he started the motor and set the boat creaming a course across a solitary stretch of sea, that for once he was seeing her as a person with moods to match his own, discovering attributes of companionship, enjoyment and spontaneity to contradict his view that she was repressed and emotionless as a puppet.

With a leap of the pulses she noted that instead of turning in the direction of home he was steering the boat onward, heading towards a spot of land on the far horizon. She relaxed, allowing a sweet sense of contentment to invade her body, a languour that retained its hold even when he reached his goal, an oasis of an island bobbing small as a cork on a vast expanse of sea, with just a few tall rocks to cast a welcome shade and a mass of seaweed strewn over a sliver of coral sand.

'My grandfather and I regarded this island as our own private retreat from the world,' he confided, swinging her out of the boat and setting her down barefoot on the sand. 'Building that hut was his idea . . .'

Birdie turned in the direction he had indicated and saw a small wooden structure no bigger than a shed, with a roof of thatched straw, a shuttered window, and three steps leading up to a wooden door.

'He was an expert at culinary improvisation,' he mused. 'Never have I tasted anything to equal his tomato, onion and fish salad eaten in the open air.'

Some sixth sense warned her that she, too, was destined never to forget this enchanted oasis tucked away behind the waves but, knowing his cynical eyes were alert for signs of panic, she suppressed all signs of alarm, even managed to mock coolly.

'There must be more than a little of the schoolboy left in any man who likes to play Robinson Crusoe—if you'll tell me what I can do to help, I'll be glad to act the role of Girl Friday!'

'You can prepare the table while I cook the fish,' he grinned, amused by the comparison. 'You'll find all the crockery you need inside the hut, but I'd advise you to wash it thoroughly, as it has not been used for some time.'

Lighting branches of shrubs to fuel the stove, he gutted the fish while she took plates, mugs and cutlery down to the sea, rinsed them well, then set them out to dry on a smooth plank of wood nailed to supports sunk into the ground adjacent to the hut, which was obviously meant to serve as a table. Two forms set either side, and a pole inserted in a hole carved out of the centre of the plank to support a straw-thatched umbrella, comprised a dining area that was unashamedly crude yet softened by a background of indescribable beauty.

While the fish were sizzling in boiling oil Vulcan went back to the boat and returned to toss her a bag full of *boccadillas*, crusty rolls which she

split, then spread with butter to accompany a dish
of tomato salad and a bottle of red wine which he
had managed to keep cool by tying string around
the neck and lowering it over the side of the boat
to dangle in deep water. By the time the meal was
ready they were too famished to spare time for
talk. Her first forkful of plump, crisply-fried
mullet was so delicious she closed her eyes to
savour fully the delicate flavour of fish enhanced
by the addition of sprigs of wild mint, then the
honey-sweet tang of huge tomatoes devilled in a
dressing of lemon juice, mustard, oil and sharp
black pepper.

Not until they were both replete, toasting each
other with their eyes across the rims of mugs
brimming with wine, did he torment her with the
lazy observation:

'I wonder if you have any idea how sensational
you look with a faded tee-shirt clinging damp
around your nipples?'

Shocked embarrassment jolted her erect, but
beneath the table their legs collided and hers
seemed struck lifeless, incapable of moving away.
Slowly, her glance locked with his, she lowered
her mug to the table, unaware that her mouth had
fallen slightly open, that a sweet bottom lip,
stained blood-red with wine, was projecting a
quivering plea for kindness. The virility projected
by a powerful, bared chest, by the contrasting
slenderness of a fine gold chain slung around a
bronzed neck, by the glint of a golden medallion
struggling to escape a mesh of fine black hairs,
stunned her senses, held her powerless in the grip
of strong sexual attraction.

'You look so innocent,' he continued musing, his eyes no longer lazy but keenly intent, 'and yet you manage to express sensuality with every feature—superb legs, beautifully soft skin, the way you unpin your hair so that it cascades down your back; supple grace, bashful eyes and a voice that echoes sweet as a cello even when you have been taunted into a small display of temper. Always you appear ladylike, yet never *inaccessible*, because something in your eyes, something about your tone of voice, suggests invitation. To put it bluntly, *querida*, the exciting message I receive is that though convention may force you to act like a lady in public, inclination could transform you into a harlot in bed!'

When lambent flame leapt to life in his eyes instinct told her that he was grappling with strong emotion, that the husky, pulsating tone of his voice was a passionate indication of violent masculine need. She saw him move swiftly towards her, guessed his intention, yet could not free her mind and limbs of paralysis in time to escape capture. His low, triumphant laughter echoed in her ears, a blurred kaleidoscope of earth, sea and sky flashed before her eyes when she was lifted from her seat, swung high into his arms, then lowered gently on to a mattress of soft seaweed.

The ardent crush of his hands upon her body, the keen hunger of his searching lips, the pressure of limbs tense and unyielding as steel unlocked within her a storm of pain and anger, the disillusionment of a woman searching for love and finding only lust.

'No . . . *no!*' she moaned, twisting out of his

grasp, 'I won't let you treat me like a mistress of the day,' she sobbed wildly, 'one of the many who are no doubt accustomed to being entertained here before being returned to their haunts in the back streets of Mahon!'

The line of his jaw tightened, betraying a whip-lashing pulse at the corner of his mouth. 'In a week we will be married,' he reminded her with angry frustration. 'In my country any wife who tries to deprive her husband of his rights is deservedly beaten!'

'Then beat me!' she sobbed, lying crushed as a flower beneath a storm of hail. 'Broken bones heal faster than the scars of sham attachment! No woman could dislike a man for loving her, *señor*,' she indicted through a haze of tears, 'but she can hate him for pretending to!'

CHAPTER ELEVEN

As the bridal car swept into the square late after-noon shadows were casting a black lacy mantle over the mellowed pink stonework of the cath-edral. A small crowd milling at the bottom of the steps cried out, '*Que mona! Muy bonita! Preciosa!*' when Birdie stepped out of the car with a grace of movement that set her satin dress shimmering from neck to hem, so that her trance-slow ascent of the cathedral steps could have been that of an apparition transported from another world, her beauty obscured by a mist of tulle.

'Are you feeling all right, Birdie?' Tony's anxi-ous eyes tried to probe behind the veil, suspicious of the misery of spirit that seemed reflected in pale, set features.

'I am now that you're here,' she tried to smile but did not quite succeed. 'I can't tell you how relieved I felt when I was told that the *Terre-à-terre* had berthed in the harbour this morning. Every bride needs the support of loved ones on her wedding day, Tony, and you and the Company are all the family I can claim. I'm so grateful to you and Lady Daphne,' she whispered, hesitating to take a deep, bracing breath as they halted before massive, widely-flung doors.

'As if anything could have kept us away once the news of your marriage reached us on the mari-time grapevine,' he scolded gruffly. 'We must have broken all records getting here in time,' he assured her, then frowned, wondering if they *had* arrived in time or just too late to discuss thoroughly the important step she was about to take, to urge her to wait until she was certain she wanted to become the wife of a man who seemed to inspire her with fear rather than love. But when a great leather curtain was pushed aside to allow them entry into the solemn interior of the cathedral; when the muted, liquid flutings of an organ ceased as if at a given signal, then suddenly recommenced playing a triumphant tribute to the approaching bride, he conceded that it was too late to counsel caution and gave all his attention to supporting the trembling, nervous girl leaning on his arm.

Concentrate hard! Birdie urged herself mentally, digging her fingers into Tony's arm. *Pretend that this is a ballet in which you are performing a starring role!*

Suddenly, sunlight through stained glass projecting splashes of topaz, silver and crimson upon grey stone walls; the upward soaring of huge marble columns that branched into mysterious arches supporting the ceiling above; the rows of pews filled with relatives and friends of the Retz family—men of rigid military bearing and women who moved and talked with the ease and simplicity of gesture associated with the aristocracy— all had their menace reduced to the familiarity of a backdrop, props, and fellow artistes. Even the leading man, waiting tall and stern at the altar rail, held no fear for her. Confidently, she relinquished her hold upon Tony's arm, turned to hand a very subdued Lucita the ivory-backed prayer book and single perfect bud of magnolia she had chosen to carry instead of a bouquet, then stepped forward with a hand outstretched into the spotlight of the grim Conde.

The performance continued without a hitch. The priest on his high altar looked magnificent in a short lace-edged surplice coloured the blue-red shade of bougainvillea flowers and a cloak of gold brocade lined with stiff green taffeta. Even the small altar boys in crimson cassocks who stepped forward on cue to hold back the corners of the priest's cloak bore without stumbling candles in silver sconces soaring two feet higher than their heads, and swung smoking censers until the smell of incense hung thick and heavy in the air.

Birdie felt proud of the way her stiff lips mimed the responses and of Vulcan's dignified bearing when he slid a wide band of gold on to her finger. Only when the finale had been reached and they turned to leave the stage did she feel that something was wrong—for although their audience had risen to its feet there was not the slightest ripple of applause!

'*Suerte!*' the crowd of wellwishers called out above the noise of traffic in the cathedral square, then waved until the car had swept El Conde and his bride away from the cathedral towards his town house where the reception was to be held.

'What are they saying?' she faltered, shy of the distinguished stranger in formal attire whom she found so hard to associate with the bare-chested rake who had seemed so set upon pre-empting their physical union just a few short days ago.

'They are wishing us luck in the game of marriage,' he told her dryly.

Birdie had thrown back the veil from her face so that the crisp tulle had formed into peaks, clustered like petals around the heart of a flower.

'Isn't marriage rather a serious occupation to be classed as a game?' she asked him timidly, unnerved by his sarcasm and by a suspicion that he had viewed the arrival of the *Terre-à-terre* as an untimely intrusion.

'You surprise me!' Black eyebrows arched, simulating astonishment. 'You appear to consider the whole of life a game and seem to be at ease only when you are playing the part of an image outside of reality. When you find sufficient courage to acknowledge your true personality, *niña*,' he leant forward to threaten, 'life will cease to be a game and you will no longer feel content to play the discarded plaything, a toy with a broken spring!'

Fortunately, as all the guests wanted to greet the new bride, she was expected to circulate through the magnificent rooms she had barely had time to glimpse during her previous visit. A buffet had been set out in a small side room and guests, chatting in sociable groups, were eating from plates containing selections of local seafood in a savoury wine sauce; sole sautéed in butter; omelettes, salads, paella, and for the nibblers a selection of *tapas*—tiny bit-size morsels of deep-fried fish and chicken—meat pastries, and saucer-size casseroles designed to fill an empty corner of the stomach between meals, before meals, or even instead of meals should circumstances warrant such deprivation.

Birdie had just slipped into a corner for a well-earned respite when Tony ran her to ground. He was holding two glasses of champagne, but though his elegant figure looked relaxed when he handed one over his eyes showed a trace of anxiety as they scoured her wan face.

'Drink this, Aurora, you look as if you are in need of a lift!'

She accepted the glass with a smile, but ignored his reference to the princess in the *Sleeping Beauty* ballet, the role that was acknowledged to be the supreme test of a ballerina in all the classical repertoire. Her own wedding was not to be celebrated with many dazzling dances, nor was there a Lilac Fairy lurking in the background, ready to cancel out the consequences of a wicked spell.

Sensing the barrier of reserve that would not allow her to confide her troubles, Tony attempted to lighten her spirits by changing the subject.

'Do you realise that I've not yet been allowed the privilege of kissing the bride?' he teased.

Even as she lifted her face to accept his affectionate kiss she glimpsed Vulcan's head turning sharply in her direction, noted the grimness of his expression as he began advancing towards her through the crowd of guests.

As if aware of scrutiny, Tony allowed his lips to linger and seemed reluctant to release her even when Vulcan's stiff presence became too obvious to be ignored. The thread of hostility that had always existed between the brilliant director and the Conde whose arrogance he abhorred became pronounced as the clashing of swords when

Vulcan's icy comment cut through their intimacy.

'An Englishman is never so natural as when he is looting—whether it be countries, cities or merely kisses!'

Birdie drew back to stare, appalled, and for the first time that day a rich tide of colour flooded her cheeks—colour that might have been mistaken for guilt. But it was anger that caused her to champion Tony, together with a resentment of having been made to feel *possessed*.

'A man cannot steal what is freely given,' she rebuked icily, then turned to bestow upon Tony a brilliant smile that misled him completely.

Impervious to undercurrents, he lifted her hand to his lips and with his glance locked with hers breathed softly: 'If only I were an artist, a composer or a poet, so that I might express a more deserving tribute to your beauty!'

'Where have you been hiding, Tony dear?' Lady Daphne descended as if on cue, just in time to defuse a potentially explosive situation. To onlookers they must have appeared an amicably chatting group, but after a quick appraisal of Vulcan's set features, Lady Daphne seemed to sense that she had barged into the midst of an area of conflict. She was carrying a plate containing a substance Birdie did not recognise, an opaque dessert that seemed to have the consistency of soft cheese, and she swiftly employed it as a form of diversion.

'Have you tried the *membrillo*?' she enquired brightly. 'If not, you should, because it's absolutely delicious on first acquaintance, although it can become a little wearisome as time goes on.'

Birdie was quick to seize the proffered lifeline. 'I haven't. What is it?'

'Quince paste, darling, a favourite Spanish dessert. Come with me, I'll get you some.'

Birdie knew she was being cowardly when she allowed Lady Daphne to lead her away, but the attitude of pretence that had bolstered her throughout the marriage ceremony was wearing very thin. Reality was beginning to loom, the realisation that her satin gown and pristine veil was no mere costume to be discarded at the end of a performance, that the lines she had delivered with such aloofness had not left her uncommitted as the reading of dialogue from a script; that tomorrow there would be no change of programme, no new scenario, no change of tempo, and that until death did them part she was to be billed with the same leading man—playing a slave cowed by her master, being forced to act as understudy to the legion of women begging to be allowed to play a starring role in his life.

Gripped firmly by the hand, she stumbled in Lady Daphne's wake and stared with dazed incomprehension when she was pushed inside an empty ante-room and heard the door being closed firmly behind her. She swung round to confront a stern-faced Lady Daphne planted like a barricade with her back against the door.

'Now,' she charged Birdie, 'I want to know exactly what's been going on since I left you in Vulcan's care. I'll be honest and admit that when I coaxed him into offering you the position as Lucita's companion I saw myself as a benevolent matchmaker bringing together two people whose relationship had got off to a bad start, but who were obviously made for each other. When news reached me of your imminent marriage I was delighted, but from the moment I set foot in the Casa de Solitario it became obvious from Vulcan's attitude and your highly nervous state that something had gone wrong. What is it, Birdie, why are you unhappy, and what lies behind Vulcan's puzzling assurances that I have no further cause for worry, that every obstacle has been cleared out of my way?'

'Is that how Vulcan sees me?' Birdie intoned stonily, her cheeks draining to the intense whiteness of her dress. 'It appears,' she choked, swinging away from Lady Daphne's too-perceptive eyes, 'that I am destined always to be treated like an unwanted parcel that keeps appearing on someone's doorstep. Vulcan coerced me into marriage because he wanted a permanent companion for Lucita, someone who could not leave at a moment's notice, and also because he saw my presence aboard your boat as a threat to your happiness. He believes, you see, that I'm in love with Tony,' she confessed simply, 'and read into your suggestion that he should offer me employment a plea for help to remove me from Tony's orbit.'

She made no attempt to break the shocked silence that followed her explanation, knowing Lady Daphne needed time to assimilate the consequences of her well-meaning interference, to recall the persuasive remarks and hints she had employed, and to realise how easily they could have been misinterpreted. Birdie waited, prepared for an apology, for an impassioned declaration that she would seek out Vulcan immediately and attempt to sort matters out, but instead she was startled by one startled, determined word.

'*Impossible!*'

'Meaning you don't believe me?' Birdie jerked round to stare.

'Meaning, my dear,' Lady Daphne countered with a conviction that was impressive, 'that you're endowing Vulcan with virtues he doesn't possess. Oh, I don't mean he's incapable of putting himself out for a friend,' she waved aside Birdie's protest, 'but not even he, chivalrous, protective, loyal though he is, would take the extreme step of sacrificing his entire future for the sake of a threatened love affair. Look at the situation from his point of view, my dear,' she urged. 'Vulcan is a virile, demanding male who works, lives and loves to a hard pattern—is such a man likely to even contemplate bondage with a wife he neither respects nor desires? Make no mistake, Birdie,' she concluded softly, 'to a Spaniard marriage is for life, so however puzzling his motives, you can be sure that from this day onwards you will rarely be allowed to stray from his side!'

Attached as closely as a prisoner to a jailor! Birdie mentally conceded, too weary to argue with the woman who seemed determined to portray Vulcan as a loving husband as opposed to a Caliph making a fresh addition to his harem. She winced from the comparison, mentally conjuring a picture of herself in surroundings of luxurious subservience, waiting with head bowed for a visit from her lord and master.

A wilful notion sprang to life, an impulse born
of inherited pride, a desire to go down fighting.
Years of training helped her to conceal an inner
shaking, to look thoughtful as if half won round
to Lady Daphne's way of thinking.

'I wonder ...' she began, then hesitated,
alarmed by her daring line of thought.

'Yes, what are you wondering, my dear?' Lady
Daphne looked hopeful. 'Have you thought of a
way I might be able to help?'

'Yes, perhaps,' Birdie gulped, then with rising
colour admitted in a rush, 'I've always worn pyja-
mas ... there's been no opportunity to shop ...
so I wondered, as you have so many glamorous
negligees, if ...'

Immediately Lady Daphne's face became
wreathed in smiles. 'My dear!' she exclaimed, her
eyes sparkling, 'I have the very thing! A delicious
concoction of chiffon and lace purchased just a
few days ago in Morocco—you can have it with
pleasure!'

Later that evening the promised parcel arrived,
long after the last of the wedding guests had
departed and Lucita had been despatched to the
Case de Solitario in Dolores' charge, consoled
with the promise of Birdie's undivided attention
once their short honeymoon in Mahon was
ended.

She was enduring the intimacy of dining alone
with Vulcan at a table bathed in the flickering
light of tall red candles set into silver sconces
when a soft-footed manservant entered the room
carrying a light, beribboned package despatched
from the *Terre-à-terre*.

'What is it?' Vulcan queried, his glance lazy yet watchful as he prowled the blush that erupted into her cheeks.

'Nothing of great importance,' she jerked guiltily, her nerves on edge, 'just a belated gift from Lady Daphne.'

'As she and Tony have already presented us with a handsome wedding present,' he drawled, flicking a glance over the beribboned package, 'one must assume that this second gift is in the nature of a honeymoon present?' He half-smiled when his guess was confirmed by her start of surprise and with his hawk eyes hooded, continued to muse: 'Honeymoon ...! Are we to share the sweet, glowing uprisal that word implies, *querida*? Or is our marriage to be soured by regret, reduced to a battleground of animosity?' Birdie stiffened with fear, caught in the beam of a swift, bright blue stare. 'A bird soon adapts to being caged, *mi cara*, can even—once its panicking wings cease to flutter—begin to enjoy the advantages of captivity.'

'Advantages?' she husked, feeling a trembling mistrust of his suavity. 'What could possibly compensate for loss of freedom?'

His mouth tightened as he studied her gracefully-poised head, her slightly bitter mouth, and eyes clouded dark with pain.

'A permanent home,' he suggested coldly, 'a mate to fulfil your needs and to supply protection; a guide to keep you on a straight course so that never again will you be tempted to commit the folly of trespassing upon unauthorised territory. Also,' he concluded meaningfully, 'a husband to satisfy the yearnings of an abandoned orphan whose sense of rejection can only be purged by the sweet penance of motherhood.'

She jumped to her feet, disturbed by his perception, agitated beyond words by his implied assumption that a wife should be grateful, obedient, adoring, submissive to her husband's demands however outrageous, however contrary to her own.

His mocking laughter followed her as she ran from the room, her flagging resolution stimulated by his scorn. During their meal she had felt herself wavering, weakened by his charm, but now she felt certain that while he had been flattering her with attention, chatting lightly to put her at her ease, he had been enjoying the taste of triumph, quietly savouring her imminent surrender. But though she had been forced to concede defeat, she planned to spoil the climax he was anticipating when Menorquin wreaked revenge upon the English by exerting superior strength until the enemy was overthrown, pinned helpless and pleading for mercy . . .

She ran inside the master bedroom, the room which for generations had been set aside by the Retz family as part of the bridal suite, keeping her eyes averted from a huge four-poster bed, its covers already turned down, awaiting its occupants, and groped along the wall for the master switch that flooded the heavily luxurious interior with light, chasing away the aura of intimacy formed by deeply shadowed corners and the pool of rose-coloured light beamed upon the bed by a solitary lamp.

Shaken by a fever of fear, she struggled out of the plain black dress she had worn during dinner, then, conscious that there was not much time left before Vulcan would be following impatiently in her footsteps, she slipped on a dressing gown, unpinned her hair, then sat down at the dressing table and pulled her theatrical make-up box towards her. Swifty, but with the skill of long practice, she began painting on a face to match the role she had been allotted.

Part of the fascination of stage make-up is the way a pretty face can be disguised to suit the image of an ugly character, the way with a few expert strokes of a brush, a few lines and smudges, an innocent expression can be transformed into common wantonness. When she had finished Birdie stared with a sort of horrified fascination at her reflection in the mirror, a face with features exaggerated in the manner she had been taught was essential if an expression is to be clearly seen on stage in a big theatre with strong lighting. Her eyes looked especially overdone, the brows thickly winging; lids sparkling with gilt, and liner forming a grotesque frame around scared eyes contrasting oddly against a flamboyantly painted mouth and a wild-silk tangle of hair.

Reluctantly she closed the lid of her make-up box, wishing there had been time to experiment with nose-putty to create a hooked nose or even a wart or two, but then reason took over—to have gone to such lengths would have been to defeat the object of the exercise, which was to disappoint the Conde by offering him not the dignified, innocent bride he was relishing but a pampered, satin-skinned, fawning *houri*!

Nervously she untied Lady Daphne's beribboned parcel, and gasped when she saw the contents. The gift could not have been more appropriate had she outlined her requirements in detail—a diaphanous nightdress and matching negligee in bold scarlet, ruffled and flounced around neck and hem, with a slashed neckline plunging down to meet a broad band of ribbon threaded through a narrow waistband.

She shivered inside its clinging folds, then without daring to glance in the mirror, grabbed the ultimate weapon—a bottle of cheap perfume that she had received as a parting gift from a hard-up colleague—and proceeded to scatter its contents indiscriminately until the atmosphere was pervaded with a sickly, overpowering scent.

It might have been its potent attack that halted Vulcan in his tracks immediately he entered the room, or perhaps it was the sight of her slim nakedness gleaming milk-white through a nightdress transformed by the beam of a solitary lamp into a cloud of scarlet gauze.

'*Muy bonita . . .!*'

Hesitantly, she turned to face the man whose cry of admiration had sounded choked, and gained the satisfaction of seeing his expression harden into lines of acute displeasure.

'*Diablo!* What have you done to your face?' he hissed, striding closer to glare with disbelief upon the painted caricature.

She trembled in his shadow, very conscious of male virility rampaging beneath a dark silk dressing gown. She tried to speak, but found that she could not. Terror was clogging her throat, her mouth felt arid, her nerves seemed attacked by some form of paralysis. She saw his dark head lift, narrow nostrils twitching as if suddenly assailed by the unpleasant scent permeating the room, then when the astonishment in his eyes was replaced by sparks of anger she knew that her message had been received and was fully understood.

'So . . .!' the softness of his tone held more menace than a shout, 'yet again you have elected to take refuge in fantasy rather than face up to reality. Will you never cease play-acting?' he grated through lips tight as a slash. 'Am I to be cursed for ever with a puppet-wife who responds only to the pull of one master?' Savage hands descended, branding the heat of frustration upon cold white shoulders. 'What conceit,' he indicted thickly, menacing closer to her quivering mouth, 'to imagine your talents are sufficient to allow you to undertake the role of houri, a woman as dedicated to her profession as any dancer, one who specialises in the art of delighting men. You have much to learn in that respect, *pajaro gris*!' He scooped her boneless body into his arms and carried her towards the bed, his dark eyes smouldering as he dropped her into a nest of pillows, then bent low to deliver a terrifying promise: 'Though inexperience is no drawback in the pursuit of knowledge, expert tuition is essential—how fortunate for you, *querida*, that you possessed wisdom enough to place yourself in the hands of a teacher who prides himself on the excellent results he obtains from his pupils!'

'THESE slippers are uncomfortable, Birdie, I can feel a blister forming on my heel!'

Birdie sighed, sensing that Lucita's fretful complaint had its basis in resentment of the fact that since her return from honeymoon in Mahon she had been too preoccupied to bestow more than half her usual attention. 'Take them off and let me look,' she responded mechanically. 'Perhaps the leather backs need bending to make them more pliable.'

'It's too hot for dancing,' Lucita sighed, sounding decidedly fractious. 'Show me again how to express feelings without the use of words.'

Birdie made a determined effort to stave off lethargy brought about by a combination of extreme heat and depressed spirits. They were nearing the end of summer, approaching the season of storms, yet the dreaded Tramontana represented no threat to a body that had survived being tossed and buffeted, had bent and writhed, clung and gasped, soared to incredible heights and plumbed new depths, during her initiation into the secret, tempestuous art of making love. In retrospect, her decision to play the role of *prostituta* in place of a shy, demure bride had been a mistake. Anger had rendered Vulcan savage, blind to terrified eyes, uncaring of panic-stricken heartbeats pounding fear through the silken-skinned *novia* crushed within the circle of his arms. But then slowly, magically, his storm of anger had abated, gripping hands had relaxed into a soothing stroke; kisses had lost their acidity and developed a probing, lingering sweetness that had caught her unawares, prompting clinging response from bruised, quivering lips.

The following hours had passed like an impossible dream in which, like the sleeping Aurora, she had been guided gently out of the dense forest of doubt that had held her prisoner, released from a limbo of frozen emotions and sent soaring on eager wings to peaks of unbelievable ecstasy. But unlike the wise thrush who sings each song twice over, Vulcan had made no attempt to recapture those wondrous moments, for since that first night of fine, careless rapture she had been left so severely alone she felt shunned, humiliated by a suspicion that far from sharing her sense of bemused happiness, he had found her gauche inexperience amusing but slightly boring.

'*Birdie . . .!*' Lucita stamped an aggravated foot, 'are you daydreaming again? Tio says that to believe in one's dreams is to spend all of one's life asleep,' she quoted importantly. 'Do waken up and see if you can guess the gestures I am miming!'

Birdie had to smile at the small, tense figure standing with hands clasped together in an unconsciously imploring gesture.

'I'm sorry, *niña*, do carry on, you have my complete attention.'

Posing vainly trying to snatch a glimpse of her reflection in the practice room mirror, Lucita lifted a hand to her eye.

'You are indicating sight,' Birdie approved, then had to strive to look solemn when Lucita clasped both hands over her heart and heaved a heavy sigh. 'Love . . .?' she suggested doubtfully.

'Yes!' Lucita cried. 'Now for the next one.' Immediately she extended her left arm and pointed to her wedding-ring finger. Birdie's eyes dropped to the heavy gold band that was Vulcan's mark of possession, the ring that indicated she was now a minor item of Retz property. 'Surely you can guess this one, Birdie?' Lucita was losing patience. 'It means marriage—love and marriage always go together!'

'Like heaven and hell?' The mocking question sent them both spinning towards the open doorway.

'Tio!' Lucita squealed with delight. 'Have you come to keep us company? We have missed you so much these past few days.'

'You must learn to speak only for yourself, *niña*,' he reproved, his smile tightening as his glance fell upon Birdie standing with hands loosely clasped, her eyes downcast in the manner of a servile *muchacha* ever conscious of the need to keep her place. 'I have neglected you both lately,' he frowned, 'but I would like to make amends by taking you with me to pay a visit to the gypsies who are gathering for a *feria* due to be held in two days' time.'

'A *feria*?' Lucita seemed barely able to contain her excitement. 'Will there be merry-go-rounds and ocean waves and stalls laden with sweets and toys and all sort of fancy goodies?'

'Unfortunately, yes . . .' Birdie looked up just in time to catch his wry grimace, '. . . together with all the ceremony traditionally associated with the position of Caixer Señor and his Señora,' he stressed, locking Birdie's glance with a bolt of mockery. 'The Caixer Señor is one who is chosen to represent the nobility at Menorquin cere-monies,' he explained gravely, 'and I'm afraid that as that duty has been allotted to me, the Señora will be expected to ride pillion dressed in a cos-tume of Old Spain.'

'Ride?' she gasped, wide-eyed with alarm. 'On a horse, do you mean?'

'On one of the proud, glossy stallions bred on the *fincas* of Andalusia,' he confirmed, twitch-ing lips giving rise to a suspicion that he was having difficulty controlling his amusement, 'but don't worry,' he hastened to assure when her smooth brow puckered, 'Lucita will show you where the costumes are kept, and I give you my solemn promise that you will not be allowed to slip out of the saddle. And now,' he dismissed the *feria* to the future and returned to debate the immediate present, 'what about our visit to the gypsy encampment—are you in favour or not?'

Although she ached to refuse, Birdie knew that the outcome of his invitation was a foregone con-clusion even before Lucita threw herself into his arms babbling excited acceptance. He allowed them time to change out of their leotards and waited by the car until they appeared on the front steps of the Casa looking cool and pretty in crisp cotton dresses.

'Would you like to sit next to me?' he invited, opening the door of the front passenger seat.

Nervously she shied from the suggestion. 'I . . . I'd better keep Lucita company in the back,' she gasped, averting her eyes from a look that was mocking her timidity, deriding her attempt to appear a closed book to the man who had delved the secrets of every page.

'Just as you wish, *querida*,' he responded politely, but in a tone so dry she was made immediately aware of her social inadequacies, was made to wonder at the conceit which for one split second had allowed her to imagine that El Conde de la Conquista de Retz had flinched from her too-hasty refusal.

He took the road that curved around the bay and set a leisurely tenor to the day by stopping at Lucita's request to allow her to watch a group of boys at play throwing hunks of bread into the crystal-clear water and then waiting expectantly for shoals of tiny fish to swarm like a flock of hungry birds, wriggling and pushing, slithering over each other's backs as the bread became lodged against a rock and they fought for a share of the prize.

When they reached the far end of the bay where the road branched left towards the capital, he took the right fork leading inland and began travelling through mainly barren hillside where tiny villages and whitewalled farmhouses surrounded by centuries-old dry-stone walls; gently sloping pine woods; olive groves, orchards, and tiny isolated churches lay slumbering beneath the heat of the sun. Occasionally they caught a glimpse of the sea and as they approached a signpost indicating a nearby cove, Lucita pleaded:

'Please, Tio, may we take a quick peep at the caves?'

'Not today, *niña*, some other time, perhaps.'

'Oh, very well,' she sighed, 'but I did so want to show Birdie where the pirate used to live.'

'You had a pirate living on your island?' Birdie queried, then immediately wondered why she should consider such knowledge surprising when she was so intimately acquainted with a looting buccaneer who would fit perfectly into the company of men who had walked planks, cut throats, drunk rum, fought duels, and deprived others of their most treasured possessions. Resentment flared in the glance she cast at his proud, dark head, then her colour rose when she caught sight of his bold glance reflected in the driving mirror and sensed the telepathic power that enabled him to delve her innermost thoughts. She was not unprepared when, with a slightly mocking edge to his tone, he confirmed her theory:

'The caves are situated on the side of a cliff that drops straight down into the sea. Legend has it that many centuries ago Menorca was constantly pillaged by Berber pirates. One day, a Berber swam ashore, the sole survivor of a pirate shipwreck, and sought refuge from hostile islanders by climbing the cliff face and using the caves as a hideout. To stave off starvation he stole from local farms, then in order to assuage an even

greater hunger he stole a Menorcan peasant girl
as well. Eventually they produced a family and it
is said that there are descendants of the Berber
living in Menorca to this day. Can you believe
that, *querida*,' he cocked a challenging eyebrow,
'or do you think the notion too far-fetched to be
true?'

'Not at all,' she assured him, managing to
achieve a tone clear and even as a cello. 'Every
cask retains some trace of the spirit it contained—
which probably helps to explain why some men's
hearts are black as pirate rum!'

She wished the words unsaid when a frown of
displeasure darkened his features and an ominous
silence fell, threatening to spoil the enjoyment of
their outing. But when the car eventually breasted
a rise and then began descending into a lush valley
where caravans resembling covered wagons had
been drawn into a circle at the edge of a stream,
her spirits rose until her excitement almost
matched Lucita's.

'Look, Birdie, there's a boy running around
with a baby pig on a leash just like a puppy!'

But as she stepped from the car Birdie's gaze
was transfixed by a group of strikingly lovely girls
wearing the traditional costume of the Spanish
gitana, colourful dresses with long tightly-fitting
bodices and skirts frilled from hip to hem; long,
narrow sleeves; embroidered three-cornered
shawls; earrings large as coins that swung and
dangled with every toss of their heads; gold
bracelets, and scarlet shoes laced above their
ankles with ribbon.

'Do they always dress so splendidly?' she

gasped, struggling to equate such finery with the rigours of outdoor living.

'No,' Vulcan's smile seemed a little less strained, 'you are about to enjoy the privilege of attending a gypsy wedding. That flower-decorated caravan set apart from the rest has been specially prepared for the newlyweds. Come!' her pulses leapt when he linked her hand in his, 'the *gitanas* have been told of our marriage and are eager to meet my bride!'

Lucita ran on in front while they began walking towards the camp. The smell of wood-smoke and the flavourful aromas drifting from cooking pots bubbling over numerous camp fires teased her nostrils, yet eager through she was to join the fascinating race of Romanies she could not resist lingering to peep into the interiors of caravans aglow with burnished copper, filled with pots of all shapes and sizes, odd items of porcelain, gaily-coloured ribbons and bunches of artificial flowers that formed part of their industry.

Immediately they were spotted stepping inside the circle formed by the caravans the gypsies cried out: '*Señor! Señora!*' and began crowding towards them with the vital, springy steps of prancing steeds, earrings and bracelets jingling, black eyes sparkling, smiling so broadly that Birdie blinked, dazzled by rows of white teeth contrasting sharply against teak brown skin.

'Ah, so *simpatica*! The *señora* is so *simpatica*! Fetch flowers—flowers, we must give her flowers!'

Seconds later her flushed cheeks and sparkling

eyes were just visible above an armful of flamboy-
ant blossoms, long-stemmed yellow and scarlet
poppies, huge, clove-scented carnations; spikes of
purple lilac, and roses, all carefully dethorned, in
shades of red, cream, yellow, and some of a shade
to rival the pink flush of pleasure rising in her
cheeks.

She sensed the scrutiny of an ancient, hawk-
eyed woman with a lined face and white hair
as she and Vulcan were led towards seats that
had obviously been reserved for guests of
honour.

'Your bride moves like a dancer with honey in
her hips, Señor Conde,' she intoned wickedly.
'Though she is not of our race, like all Spanish
women she was born to love and be loved—so
why does she limp, *señor*, and why does her
heart ache even more than the pain in her
ankle?'

Sensing from Birdie's heightened colour and
from the grim tightening of Vulcan's features that
his mother's blunt question had caused them
embarrassment, the chief of the tribe quickly
intervened by striding forward carrying a little
wooden basket containing drinking glasses and an
enormous wickercased bottle of wine.

'No, *muchas gracias!*' Birdie refused, feeling
that the drink would choke her.

'*Si, si, si!*' he smilingly insisted, leaving her no
option but to acknowledge his gesture of hospitality.

As soon as Vulcan raised his glass and gravely
toasted: '*Saludo!*' every sleek-haired, level-eyed
man responded. Then guitars began to twang and

music, thrumming as wind captured between high, narrow walls, escalated until the air vibrated with the clapping and shouting of gypsies inciting the musicians to even noisier efforts.

Then with startling suddenness the guitars fell silent, the noise died, and a girl sidled into the circle of onlookers, sat down upon the ground, then demure and unselfconscious as a child began to sing. Her voice was so exquisite that even the children stopped scuffling and dogs padding silently around the perimeter of the camp became strangely still.

From the passionate notes, the anguish portrayed on the singer's face, Birdie judged that she was singing a song to her lover, an impassioned message that Vulcan seemed anxious to impart when he bent his dark head to translate softly against her ear:

'Love must be like the blowing wind, fresh and invigorating.
Capture the wind within walls and it becomes stale.
Open tents, open hearts; let the wind blow!'

She did not dare look up nor turn towards him, would not allow herself to be deceived yet again by the master of the *piropos,* to have her head turned by flattery she knew to be false, casual, meaningless phrases that had little to do with sincerity and even less to do with love. As a defence for panic-stricken pulses, for a heart hammering frantically as a captive on the door of a cell, she retreated behind a barrier of reserve, a curtain of ice that had to appear impenetrable even though at the slightest pressure it would give way.

Keeping her eyes averted from the tutor whose face had haunted her dreams ever since the night he had accepted her as a pupil, she forced stiff lips to murmur: 'Forgive my reluctance to continue with the sort of lesson you teach, *señor*; I prefer to remain faithful to my own ideals, however misguided and naïve, rather than learn from the faithless about love's tragedies.'

He was too self-controlled, too alert to the possibility of attracting the attention of one of the gypsy tribe to betray anger, but the grip he fastened upon her wrist was agonising when he hissed:

'I suspect that you are the type of pupil who needs to hear a lesson repeated a great number of times before its meaning becomes obvious, in which case the obligations imposed by vows of matrimony may become stamped upon your conscience the second time around!'

Her startled head jerked upwards, but just as she was about to demand an explanation the girl's singing ceased and immediately a fiddler began to play. As the youngsters of the tribe jumped to their feet and began dancing hilariously she noticed their widely grinning chief approaching carrying two red kerchiefs and watched bewildered while Vulcan accepted one and tied it around his neck. When the beaming chief turned to her and offered the remaining kerchief she felt she had no option but to follow Vulcan's example.

'You are now formally betrothed in accordance with Romany custom,' the chief shocked her by saying. 'May I say, on behalf of my tribe, how honoured you and the Señor Conde have made us feel by looking with favour upon our suggestion that you should marry a second time in the manner of the gypsies? Your acceptance of the kerchief was a public admission of the love you feel for your bridegroom, and now all that remains is for us to agree the dowry payment before the actual marriage ceremony is performed. With your permission, *señora*, I will take upon myself the duties of your father.'

Feeling trapped, made furious by Vulcan's wicked, unrepentant smile, Birdie gave a choked gasp which the chief immediately interpreted as agreement. Folding his arms across his chest, he turned towards Vulcan and waited, adopting the stance of a father determined to get the best possible deal for his marriageable daughter.

Solemnly, but with a twinkle in his eyes that only she could read, Vulcan opened the negotiations in the time-honoured gypsy way.

'I have lost a little cow!'

The chief nodded briefly. 'You can have the lost one in exchange for ten gold coins.'

To her intense annoyance, Vulcan piled on humiliation by pretending to take time to consider, slowly eyeing the glossy hair, the bright eyes, the indignantly-flaring nostrils and every shapely curve of the healthy little cow for which he was bidding. Finally, frowning as if suspicious of being cheated, he concluded the deal:

'Agreed!'

With a grin of triumph the chief clasped him by the hand before twirling to yell an order to the dancing tribe. Abruptly the music ceased, and the members of the tribe hurriedly arranged themselves in two opposite rows about six feet apart. Halfway down between the rows two gypsies held a broomstick about a foot above the ground and in response to a call from the chief, Vulcan, with the rakish red kerchief still tied around his neck, walked down the row, jumped over the broomstick, paused, then swung round to face Birdie, who had been positioned ready to take her turn.

Slowly, showing a reluctance that delighted the race of people to whom the modesty of women was of paramount importance, she advanced between the line of gypsies and jumped over the broomstick, straight into her bridegroom's outstretched arms.

'*Ne! Kana romadi san!*' The cry rang out from the throats of the tribe.

'*There now!*' Vulcan translated gravely as he slid a rush-ring next to the heavy gold band on her wedding-ring finger, '*you are truly married!*'

Lusty cheering rose above the sound of music and stomping feet as he swept her off her feet and began running the gauntlet of the cheering, back-slapping tribe.

'Put me down!' she insisted furiously, fighting to wriggle out of his grasp as he carried her towards the isolated caravan he had implied had been decorated with flowers for the benefit of some anonymous bridal couple. But with a throaty chuckle that filled her with misgiving he mounted the steps, strode inside the caravan, and kicked shut the door.

She froze to stillness in his arms, sensing the intent behind eyes aflame with impatient desire for the wife whose body he held in bondage but whose spirit he could not chain.

'This is our private place where we can laugh and cry together, *mi cara*,' he husked, lowering her gently on to a mattress scented with herbs— rue, the bitter herb used by Romanies as a symbol of repentance, the herb that was said to purge and purify and was even believed capable of casting out the devil.

'Is there no limit to your trickery?' she accused, her eyes hurt as a child mourning over some sore place. 'You seem to enjoy seeing me humiliated, treating me in turn as a servant, a thief, a slave girl and now,' she shuddered with distaste, 'as a bartered cow!'

'The blame for such confusion lies entirely with you, *preciosa*,' he countered thickly. 'I, too, am tired of playing Hunt the Lady, of being kept at arm's length, of being married to a succession of fictitious heroines whose characters you hide behind because you are dissatisfied with your own personality! Did you think I was unaware that even on our wedding day you were playing a role, that the vows you spoke meant less than nothing to you? I want a flesh and blood wife,' he stressed roughly. 'I want to feel your warm, silken body quivering beneath mine . . .' His lips descended to search for the velvet soft hollow at the base of her throat, then lingered, captivated by a wildly fluttering pulse.

'Why should the outcome of a second marriage of convenience turn out to be any different from the first?' she cried bitterly, her voice breaking on a sob. 'The motive remains the same . . .'

'Not quite,' he contradicted hoarsely, 'because this time, *querida*, my motive is revenge, revenge for many sleepless nights during which I have been forced to relive the torture of your contempt, the humiliation of being *tolerated*! This time I mean to be patient, to wait until your passions are inflamed, until your eyes are pleading, your lips aching to be kissed! Not until you beg my forgiveness will I even attempt to relieve the agony of desire with the soothing balm of love, for then, and only then, will I be certain that my thistle-down wife—blown back and forth on the winds of insecurity—has sown her last seed of doubt, is ready to put down roots and to blossom into beautiful maturity!'

CHAPTER THIRTEEN

IT was the day of the *feria*, the day when the bride of the Caixer Señor was to be paraded before the happy, rejoicing crowds thronging the streets of the capital. For two days Lucita had deliberated over which costume to choose from many stored from the past in sandalwood boxes and examined meticulously by Dolores and her seamstresses in order to keep deterioration at bay.

Predictably, Lucita had fallen in love with a buttercup frilled crinoline with a miniature green shoulder-shawl and a matching rounded comb that towered importantly above her mass of dark curls when, miraculously, Birdie had managed to arrange it so that the comb remained fixed and upright on her small proud head. The tottering but splendid little *damisela* had departed some time ago to seek the approval of her beloved *Tio*, and now, Birdie reluctantly conceded, the time had arrived when she, too, must brave the scrutiny of the husband whose company she had deliberately avoided since the day of their gypsy wedding.

She braced for disapproval, and without a glance towards the magnificent satin gown, the hand-made shawl embroidered with huge scarlet peonies, the lace mantilla, discarded at the last moment in favour of a costume more in keeping with her subdued mood, she hurried out of her bedroom and downstairs to the study where she knew Vulcan would be waiting.

She swallowed hard when, in response to her knock, a deep voice responded: '*Adelante!*' and gasped when she stepped inside the room, her heart jolted by the impact of Vulcan's lithe, imposing figure clad in the manner of the *caballeros*, with a black, tight-fitting jacket set upon straight shoulders. Black sword-slim corduroy pants with a scarlet sash swathed around narrow hips, and a black Cordoba hat usually worn straight but which momentarily he had tipped to the back of his head. After a swift, startled appraisal her glance dropped to the ground as she fought to suppress a wild rush of colour imposed by remembered shame.

'Why are you trembling, *cara?*' The question smouldered dangerously as the eyes that had raked her from head to toe the moment she entered the room. 'Is it because you have deliberately chosen to dress in a manner you imagined I would find displeasing? If that was your aim then you have not succeeded, for contrarily, a woman dressed in masculine attire is made to appear infinitely appealing, exquisitely feminine, and,' his voice developed the black velvet intensity of his outfit, 'utterly desirable.'

Birdie hung her head, lashes throwing a gold-tipped screen over eyes dark with shame as slowly and thoroughly he examined the long black riding skirt and shining leather boots, the short Spanish jacket cut on masculine lines, the high white stock, and the wide-brimmed sombrero she was threading through nervous fingers.

'*Muy guapa!*' he complimented with such graity she felt impelled to raise her head. 'You will appeal as a charming novelty compared with the majority of girls who favour clinging gowns decked with frills and flounces.'

She smothered a cry and was moved almost to the point of forgiveness when she glimpsed a ghost of pain reflecting in his dark eyes, a remnant of the revenge she had unintentionally managed to inflict when, after gaining every victory he had promised would occur within the walls of the private place the Romanies had set aside for them to laugh and cry together, after the sweet torture of his teasing kisses and seductive caresses had turned her wanton, begging for his forgiveness and his love, sanity had dawned and jerked from her cold lips the shamed, whispered admission that had changed his warm, perspiring body to stone.

'Sometimes, in the darkest moments of my life, I begin to wonder if God really does exist!'

'Please don't look so sad, little lame bird!' He broke her trance by reaching out to gently tilt her chin. 'Grant me the pleasure of your company for just one more day and in exchange I promise that you shall have your freedom. I have treated you very badly,' he admitted with the sombreness of a man who has spent many bitter hours reflecting upon his faults, 'it is my dearest hope that in time you might find it possible to forgive me. Meanwhile,' he sighed with a finality that squeezed every drop of blood from her heart, 'as I have been forced to acknowledge the futility of expecting affection to flourish behind the bars of conscience and duty, I have decided that the *pajarita* must be set free and allowed to fly back to the nest she has always looked upon as home. I shall try to make this last day a happy one, *querida*,' he lifted her hand to his lips and kissed each fingertip one by one, 'so that when you leave you will take with you at least one memory that can be recalled with pleasure—a parting gift of laughter to help cancel out the tears.'

As he led her outside to the front of the *casa* she was battling with a gamut of conflicting emotions. His sudden *volte-face* had taken her completely by surprise, so assured had she been, so conditioned to the idea of spending the rest of her life in his demanding, aggravating, often hurtful but always exhilarating company. Her dazed mind could not accept the fact that from tomorrow onwards she would no longer be called upon to battle against his mastery, to guard her heart, her actions, her expressive face and impulsive words from betraying the love whose roots had sprung from a tiny seed and then strengthened, inch by inch, day by day, until it had become a firmly established, integral part of her being.

A groom was waiting at the bottom of the steps holding the reins of a frisky Spanish steed, prancing proudly as if conscious of being groomed for a special occasion that had called for its docked tail to be bound with primrose satin, for its bridle to be decked with swansdown rosettes, for saddlecloths and trappings of scarlet and green, breeching straps embroidered with coloured silks, stirrups following the pattern of the ancient Moor's and for the fringed

...ather *chaparajos* favoured especially by the *caballeros*.

'Usually, the *novias* prefer to perch on the *almo-hada*—a long bolster-like cushion that is flung across the horse's haunches—in order to display their dresses to advantage,' Vulcan explained as he vaulted into the saddle and held out encouraging arms, 'but because you are sensibly dressed I will sit you in front of me where you will be safer.'

Safe was hardly the word Birdie would have used to describe her condition when with the help of the groom Vulcan lifted her aloft and set her down in the saddle a-pillion so that his chest was her backrest and strong forearms pressed either side of her waist when he tightened his grip upon the reins.

'*Viva! Viva!*' the groom called out as he slapped the horse's hindquarters to speed it on its way. In spite of her determination not to show fear, Birdie screamed when the prancing animal reared slightly before setting off to trot down the length of the driveway.

'Don't be afraid!' She knew from the tone of Vulcan's voice that he was smiling. 'I'll keep you safe——' Then, as if recalling his earlier promise, he breathed an afterthought that drew tears of pure misery to her eyes: '. . . that is, for the short time that I am to be permitted.'

Desperately she twisted round in the saddle to face him and would have been appalled at the notion that the glint in tear-wet eyes could have been mistaken for a sparkle of joy. 'You have definitely decided that I must leave, Vulcan . . .

there is no possible chance that you might change your mind?'

The haughty *caballero* drew himself tall. 'I have definitely decided,' he confirmed stiffly. 'You need have no fear that I will go back on my word!'

The road leading towards the capital was choked with traffic, motorcars and lorries; horses, mules and donkeys; tandems and gypsy caravans as well as hundreds of laughing, excited people on foot, all eagerly anticipating the *feria* that might last for one day or even three.

Many people hailed them as they entered the city engulfed in festival fever and as they rode through narrow streets lined with pretty white-washed houses their occupants leant from balconies adorned with iron filigree work to toss blossoms into the crowd and to press glasses of sherry upon thirsty passers-by. The sound of rich, vibrant flamenco music filled the main square that had been turned into a playground lined with avenues of stalls laden with sweets, china, children's toys, fancy gifts, wines and good things to eat, and paper flowers fluttered from the roofs of striped tents fitted out with wooden floors that were already reverberating to the tempo of dancing feet.

In spite of her heavy heart, Birdie's eyes were shining with excitement when she twisted round to gasp: 'How wonderful to see so many people looking so happy!'

Vulcan's arms tightened around her waist, but though he returned her smile his eyes retained